JAN BALABÁN

MAYBE WE'RE LEAVING

TRANSLATED BY CHARLES S. KRASZEWSKI

TRANSLATION OF THIS BOOK WAS SUPPORTED BY

GLAGOSLAV PUBLICATIONS

MAYBE WE'RE LEAVING

by Jan Balabán

Translated from the Czech and introduced
by Charles S. Kraszewski

Translation of this book was supported
by the Ministry of Culture of the Czech Republic

Book cover and interior design by Max Mendor

Publishers Maxim Hodak & Max Mendor

www.glagoslav.com

ISBN: 978-1-911414-69-8

A catalogue record for this book is available from the British Library.

CONTENTS

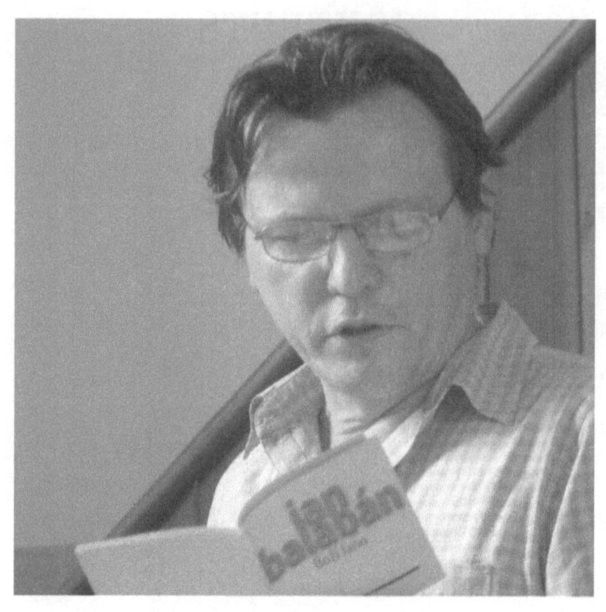

JAN BALABÁN

1961 – 2010

WHO IS THE THIRD THAT WALKS ALWAYS BESIDE YOU?

The Everyday Apocalypse
in Jan Balabán's Maybe We're Leaving.

Two great Christian authors come to mind when one considers the stories that make up the present volume: Fyodor Dostoevsky and T.S. Eliot. The first is directly apparent: Pavla, the young girl renting a cottage from the hulking tippler Vladek in the story "Bottoms Up," fears that one night he'll come into the apartment she shares with Ivan and kill them both with his hatchet "like that Karamazov fellow." "Raskolnikov," Ivan corrects her calmly — she'd mistaken *Crime and Punishment* for *The Brothers Karamazov*. Then, in "Edita," when Vladimír gets out of bed to rush cross town and pick up his unfaithful wife, he wonders bitterly, "Who am I, Prince Myshkin?" referencing the pure Christian hero of *The Idiot*.

Eliot, on the other hand, is present only indirectly, yet for all that, in a much deeper way. Whether or not Balabán was influenced by the great Anglo-Catholic poet, their work springs from the same conviction: this world, and the stream of time inseparable from it, are things lent us. We need to be aware of the necessity of right action, while we *can* act, in order to live a fully human life and — hopefully, attain an even fuller life on the other side of the grave that awaits us. Even the slightest act here below is freighted with an eternal significance for good, or evil, as Eliot says. A life worth living — or, rather, worthily lived — is one that is lived in conscious awareness of this fact, one in which the human agent strives to do good for others, and, ultimately, for himself. The time-centred words of John 9:4 are not among the sparse Biblical citations that we find in Balabán's stories: "I must work the works of Him that sent me, whilst it is day: the night cometh, when no man can work." However, they perfectly sum up the entirety of Eliot's corpus, and the book in hand, as well. They are at the heart, I submit, of the book's title: *Možná, že odcházíme* — *Maybe We're Leaving*; a curious phrase, but one which carries an implicit weight of consequence that is apparent at first contact, and even more suggestive after one reads through the entire collection. The title might also be translated *It's Possible, that We're Passing Away,* and this, with the subtle lyricism that is characteristic of Balabán's prose, strikes one as an introductory clause that demands its completion in the reader's mind: "and therefore…"

Balabán has a poetic gift which Eliot would certainly have appreciated. In the original Czech his prose is lucid, suggestive, and evocative with an immediacy, a conciseness, usually reserved for verse. Petr Hruška speaks of his "ability for precise, pregnant definitions [which is] well complemented by a talent for the creation of completely fresh poetic images."[1] Unsure as to whether this comes across adequately in my English translation, I will yet be bold enough to submit at least a short example from "Salami Horses":

> The road narrowed to a pathway leading into the midst of the riverside forest. Huge trees: lindens, alders, maples, oaks and innumerable hornbeams enclosed them in a balmy twilight. The path twisted and turned in the thick undergrowth of bear garlic, the white flowers of which twinkled like sparks.

It is a striking synaesthesia — one can almost hear and smell that bear garlic, as well as see it. It is an expression not unlike what we find in the verse of Marianne Moore, whom Eliot greatly appreciated (and who also had a penchant for the building up of crescendos of images).

But again, it is the message of imminent responsibility that most links Balabán with Eliot. Stylistically, besides the obvious generic differences, he is closer in literary approach to the great realists and psychological novelists of the European nineteenth century, chief

---

1   In his note on the author accompanying *Balabán. Povídky* (Brno: Host, 2010), p. 517. In another short essay, he writes: "His text develops from an incisive feeling for details, for small events, actually rather a mere episode, but always bound to a concrete person in a concrete time and space, in a concrete life-situation, from which it is possible to emerge only by progressing in the direction of some sort of attempt at generalisation." "Vážně," also in *Balabán. Povídky,* p. 512.

among whom is Fyodor Dostoevsky.[2] The quote here to offer is the fevered reflection of Oldřich from "And the Birds as Well," who tries to shield his mind from the terrors of his ornithophobia by an abstract consideration of the child in his wife's womb, the gender of whom they do not yet know:

> *And so thus must you address twice over one incomprehensible child. They are two approaches to one summit, to the abstract child, of whom all concrete newborns are just imperfect variants, just like all people are merely unsuccessful derivatives of man, of the son of man, the pattern elevated above the poverty of all concrete names, above all vain human destinies.*

This is an odd, yet torturously logical, meditation (which began with a philological consideration of the morphology of the names Andrea/Ondřej) that would not be out of place in the mouth of one of the great Russian's hyper-intellectual heroes, like Ivan Karamazov, during his disquisition on the Grand Inquisitor. Yet Balabán is nowhere near as drastic as Dostoevsky. Violence, up to and including brutal murders, occurs in all three of the novels referenced in the pages of this book, but the Czech author does not need to resort to overwhelming shock tactics to discuss the pathologies of everyday life.[3] For these are quotidian situations we are presented with in *Maybe We're Leaving*. They range from the nervy half-bitten anxieties of a couple in a second marriage, played out in front of a foundling dog ("His Master's Voice") to the heartrendingly tragic, yet no less common, situation of a child suffering from an incurable illness ("The Burning Child"), but they are all of them stories to which we can all relate. They are so common in their conception that each reader, I reckon, has heard of something similar happening in the "real life" that surrounds her or him, and

---

2   Hruška notes this as well, referring to "his extraordinary degree of seriousness, degree of gravity found in his words. It reminds one of that evangelical vigour in which narratives of time past are written, in the age of the Russian realist novels." p. 514.

3   Physical violence in the context of marriages breaking down, or, rather, its allure and repulsiveness to the characters concerned, can be found in stories such as "Uršula" and "Edita." But that is about as far as it goes.

even possibly — though one hopes it is not so — has experienced it on his own skin.

The limpid descriptions of these everyday situations create a sense of reality that drives deeper than what we find in the great novels of nineteenth century Realism. Objects so common that they are within our reach at this moment, as we hold this book in our hands, and people so common as to be our neighbours, coupled with Balabán's poetic mixing of narrators from third-person omniscient to stream-of-consciousness first person,[4] foster in us a sense of lived immediacy which forbids us to hold the situations at arm's length. We can almost taste the stories. As Hruška so accurately describes it in the above note, Balabán progresses from minute detail to generalisation, and thus effects a very human expansion of the experience from what happened to this particular individual, to something that touches upon us all, as humans.

The intimacy of the narrative is also helped on by the interwoven structure of Balabán's collection. Many, but not all, of the stories are linked. They do not run into one another consecutively, as they might in a traditional frame narrative; they are linked, rather, by the author's use of the same characters in different stories. Dr. Roman Hradílek is little more than an introductory prop for the story of his wife in "Uršula," while he is front and centre in "Salami Horses," and appears as a much more sympathetic character than we would have expected, based on the first tale. Likewise, his wife is only tangentially mentioned in his story — providing another look at the character of that protagonist, with whom we sympathised in "Uršula," and their son Robert, barely mentioned in the earlier work, is fleshed out and made real in the latter. The despairing drunk of "Emil" makes a phantom appearance in "Bottoms Up," while the dysfunctional Červenka clan to whom we are introduced at second-hand in "The Cedar and the Hammer" make a guest appearance, drunk at the counter of the liquor store, near the conclusion of "Emil." The positive young lovers Gabriela and Timi thread through both "Gabriela" and "Ray Bradbury." The effect we experience when coming across these familiar characters at unsuspected moments is not unlike that achieved by Krzysztof Kieślowski in his own interplaiting cinematic series *Dekalog*.

---

4 The latter is indicated in our translation by italics.

Since all of his stories take place in Ostrava and its general environs, Balabán heightens the reality of his narratives by immersing the reader in a situation that approximates life in a common area. We become the neighbours of these people, and they bob and weave into and out of our purview just as do the familiar faces of our apartment block, our workplace, our parks and the hospitals we visit. Unlike the writer he surely admired, Balabán does not introduce any feverish Raskolnikov into his stories, who butchers a defenceless old woman in order to test out a philosophical thesis. The anguish of a single mother about to introduce her child to an apartment in a housing estate that, with its defensively barred windows, seems more like a prison cell than a real home ("Magda"), is enough to arouse our sympathies and engage our minds on questions concerning the world about us, and the social conditions in which some of us are forced to live. By focusing our eyes on the everyday concerns and mundane trials of common, ordinary individuals — whose stories we are sometimes led to consider from more than one angle, as in the case of Roman and Uršula — Balabán slyly engages our sympathy on behalf of quite unremarkable people. And in so doing, he displays a great, deep, Christian humanism, which leads us to acknowledge the worth and dignity of every single human being.

Jan Balabán (1961—2010) was only eight years old when Aleksander Dubček sought to introduce "Socialism with a human face," a less repressive, open rule in the then-Communist controlled Czechoslovak Socialist Republic. He was still eight years old when the Soviet Union, the Communist hegemon of Eastern Europe, led the armies of five "fraternal" Communist nations into Czechoslovakia, in order to repress the Prague Spring and reintroduce totalitarian order. It is worth considering whether this wrenching event — the excitement of a Western nation beginning to breathe with both lungs again, suddenly stifled under the Soviet boot — had a seminal influence on the young boy's developing consciousness. Certainly, the characters in all of the short stories that make up *Maybe We're Leaving* seem to be in search of something that was taken away from them, to return to a better world that existed just around the corner they turned a moment before. Whether it be Edita's husband, heading for a messy divorce, yet desperately nostalgic for the happy times of their marriage, little, terminally-ill Katka longing for that time before she learned how to count, which conflates in her mind with the time before she grew sick, or the nerdy Jaromír, sighing after the pristine Pre-Cambrian era, unspoilt as yet by the hand of man, each and every actor on the stage of Balabán's collection is in search of a return path to a paradise lost. "She didn't understand what she was supposed to understand," the narrator of "The Burning Child" tells us, in reference to Katka, sick in hospital, and preternaturally talented with a mathematical sharpness that holds her in an obsessive grip, she merely nodded so that she could get up from her crouch at last and continue on the path between the pines leading to the ruins on that hot summer day, which she still remembered chiefly as *back then*, when she still didn't know how to count. Somewhere in the back of her head she still preserved the image of her incomprehension, when she saw those lines or pebbles checked or crossed in front of her eyes as nothing more than lines or pebbles. In the same way, she remembered the incomprehensible shapes of the letters in their rows on the signs. They were not yet words and letters, but a mystery. Now, at ten years old, she guarded these memories of her illiteracy and innumeracy like a treasure chest, containing her real childhood.

Children play an important role in these stories. Most often, they facilitate the familiar theme of childhood as a period of innocence, or at least something *better* than the modern world: that golden age of mankind dimly remembered, to which there is no way back. In "Magda," young Jaromír stumbles across a pristine oak-grove which provides him with an oasis in the midst of a brutal and cold life in the concrete pre-fabs of Ostrava: "*Dubovina. Yes, Dubovina, Dubovina!* This was for him alone — no one else knew anything about it — about that shade stretching up to the heavens, about those trunks as massive as the piers of a church." The contact is so visceral, that he even names the spot — in a way not unlike the "Goldengrove" of Gerard Manley Hopkins' weeping Margaret. The naming of a place is a taking possession of it, and this Goldengrove, this Dubovina, will be "unleaving" in the best sense of the word used by the punning British poet. Jaromír will grow up and leave it — to his detriment and regret — when he enters adulthood. Yet Dubovina itself, part of that natural world which Balabán describes so poetically and lovingly in the pages of his book, will remain, and retain its healing might. Twenty years, at least, pass between Jaromír's story and that of Magda, the eponymous hero of the narrative. Ugly apartment blocks now stand where the acres of maize fields stretched before the boy's eyes, and the mysterious airplane hangar, which made him shiver, has been gutted of all its numen via its conversion into a supermarket. But Dubovina remains as an oasis amidst it all:

> She lights a cigarette and balls herself up into the intimate area bordered by her shoulders and knees, collarbones, small breasts, lap and arms. *Here I'm home. Here I'll make your crib, little boy.* She smokes and sobs a little bit. *We'll go to the discount store in the old hangar together, shopping. You'll like the arches. And on our walks we'll make a little detour into that little wood of oaks, all shattered and bruised, left among the prefabs. There nobody'll find us.*

Impermanence, mutability, the stream of time, which carries everything — but especially the good things, the ones we regret — away from us, never to be found again, is the defining characteristic of these stories. It is tempting to see here an almost Ovidian sense of the worsening of times. Men, and the civilisations they created, were better "back then;" the modern world is soulless, empty. This idea can certainly be found in the reflections of Hans, upon his arrival at his grandfather's old parish to collect some books, while the most recent pastor and his wife are moving out: "He noticed that the large Volvo was now almost full — such as contemporary churches never are. Soon the pastor and his wife would be off, and the vicarage would be orphaned. They call it an unstaffed parish." The church is no longer needed, and where it is allowed to serve its dwindling congregations, even its architectural decoration has been pared back to the absolute minimum.

Similarly, Vladek, the hero of "Bottoms Up," compares the capable, tough and fruitful generation of his grandparents with the grubby and devolved state of his own:

> Granddad walked the seven kilometres into the village each Sunday to Mass, in a black suit with a hat on his head. That suit can still be found in the cabinet. Vladek wouldn't be able to squeeze himself into it, even if he tried. Narrow arms, short pant legs — what a small fellow he had been. When he thought

of it from time to time, Vladek just couldn't understand how such small people (Grandma was a full head shorter than her husband) could bear so much work. And everything by hand — no chainsaw, no winch to pull the wood close. *Those were solid people. Unbelievable people*, their grandson thought, shaking his head. *Everything in good order, washed and swept clean, not like it is with me.*

Man has grown smaller, as have his ambitions and opportunities. The cynical number cruncher in "Bethesda" describes his own downward spiral:

> Once he had studied music, then even theology — he had this twisted period in his life, when he wanted to "serve" — and in the end, he finished in this well-paying, but gruelling grind at the computer. At work, he had to forget completely about everything, switch off all unnecessary circuitry and concentrate only on what the computer wanted of him.

The urge to "serve" is encased in quotation marks here, because it seems to the person concerned that such dreams are not only out of step with real life, but the domain of such mousy, do-gooder souls as are themselves in need of charity. He's wised up, so it seems. Yet how has he progressed since those unprofitable days of impractical pursuits? Turning from the vocations of musician and pastor of souls, he has become the slave of the computer, attentive only to what it "wants of him:"

> *Where are my numbers? They have disappeared into the underworld of forgetfulness like unplayed notes. I am paid to shuffle thousands of numbers through my poor brain, numbers of which I know nothing.. I'm like the musical scribes, who made copies of scores they never heard. No one wanted them to hear them. They might as well have been deaf. All that was required of them was clean penmanship, and thus in their ignorance they touched the summits of the musical art. They say that the entire Gospel can be found in the compositions of Johann Sebastian, and in their heads nothing more remained than there does in mine after the passage of these numbers.*

But the characters who populate Jan Balabán's stories are not victims. From this statement we except children, of course, and animals, of which Balabán was inordinately fond and which he describes with touching empathy. Examples of this abound; we shall focus on only two. In "His Master's Voice," the Catholic Anna Maria is irritated with her Protestant husband's sermon to the dog in the foyer, which strikes her as overbearing and nastily triumphalist, exploitative:

> Beyond confessional distinctions, though, what really bugged her was the way her husband, in his hangover, exalted himself above the dog, as if it were a mere worm. Who else would seek to assert his dignity above that of an unfortunate, stray animal, and in such a refined way, as if he expected a confession of solidarity and understanding?

Call him a tree-hugger if you must, but the sensitive appreciation shown to animals by Balabán in his stories — the understated sorrow for the "salami horses" leaps out at us — is no mere cuddliness. It serves a subtle, yet strong, philosophical purpose. Oldřich, the male protagonist of "And the Birds as Well," is literally prostrate with an irrational fear of birds. The only manner in which he can rid himself of it, is by slaughtering a tom turkey at a farm. He pushes himself to do it, and it works. He returns to his job as a ship designer, and rejoins his wife and unborn child in normal life. However, in the end, although he seems to be healed of ornithophobia, he may well have replaced that hang-up with something worse:

> The aft superstructure with rudder bracket and rudder post of the transatlantic ship was assuming clear contours on his computer, thanks to his precise calculations. Everything was in order, as much as anything can be. Only from time to time did his heart pain him on behalf of that heart, which had been beating so close to his own heart, and then ceased beating.

The economical image of that still-beating heart which he felt thumping against his own chest before he ended its pulsing, by hacking off the animal's head on the chopping block, is so immediate and evocative that further commentary is unnecessary. But the point is, whatever

Balabán's convictions in regard to animal welfare may have been, the sympathy he reveals in these concluding lines are more on the side of the turkey than the man. Oldřich goes from being a victim to a killer. He even comes to the realisation that it was not birds he had a problem with, really, but killing. Cruelly persecuted throughout the entire story (by his own mind), he is freed of that persecution by becoming a persecutor himself. Killing, as therapy? Killing, as a constituent element of human nature, the lack of which leads to illness? This sort of Darwinistic, law-of-the-jungle world does not agree with Balabán's ethos. And just as, stylistically, he progresses from concentration on individual details to metaphors open to and descriptive of us all, in these stories, Mankind's bloody dominion over the animal world becomes a topic inciting us to consider Man as a bloody creature. From stories of animal cruelty, we are moved to questions of man's inborn cruelty to others, and from that unsavoury thought, to a consideration of how we might better ourselves, and our world, by a realisation of the imperative to gentleness and understanding for all — including, and perhaps especially, other human beings.

Children and animals are innocent; children and animals can be, and sometimes are, victimised on the pages of *Maybe We're Leaving*. It's not that way with the adult characters, who are truly responsible for the fixes they find themselves in. However, if there were any one among them who might justly gripe against the way in which his life has been skewed and corrupted by his early environment, that would be the hero of "At the Communists." A Freudian tale if there ever was one, "At the Communists" grounds the adult Leoš's problems in his upbringing, at the hands of an overbearing mother, who "knowing what is best for everybody," not only jammed him into the strictures of a Communist childhood from which most parents sought to shield their sons and daughters, but ostentatiously performed sex acts in front of the child, despite her husband's prudent objections. Why she did this — whether it was perverted exhibitionism, or a no-less unfitting didacticism, aimed at depriving sex of its prurient mysteries in the child's mind — is never quite explained. It is, however, a rape. By imperiously forbidding the teenaged Leoš to leave the common bedroom for the kitchen once the moaning in the conjugal bed has begun, the wicked mother is using sex as a tool of control, of power. But the fact remains that although Leoš is able, and more than willing, to castigate his mother's actions, as an adult, he is no different:

> *To calmly buy yourself a bottle of good Hungarian wine, sure, Egri Bikavér, and drink it, alone if you must, or with a female, whom you lead to the door tomorrow, with a smile, and close it behind her. All right. With a smile and a little something else, I don't have anything else for you, but what I gave you is quite enough. Three times a night, for sure. Four, no problem.* That's why he bought himself a nice wide bed. A real airport for long taxiing and sheer takeoffs. *It depends on what you're flying. I fly all sorts: from ultra-lights to B-52s. I've got something for them all. But mostly I prefer the F-16s, oh, those young rockets! — you can do whatever you like with them. They respond so well.*

His attitude toward sex is no better than his mother's. He completely objectifies his partners, to the extent that he not only pays for services rendered, but spins out a metaphor of womanhood that deprives the girls of their humanity. The bed is an airport runway; the women are categorised as airplanes, and he is the pilot — completely in charge of the experience, which is entirely for his benefit, as he conducts his aerial acrobatics at the controls of the passive machines.

Love is a problematical thing in the stories that make up *Maybe We're Leaving*. There is hardly a single instance of a truly happy pair of lovers in its pages. Divorce, infidelity, and unhappiness are the norm. Twice — in "Uršula" and "Edita" — violent marital spats are preludes to hateful sexual relations. In "And the Birds as Well," where we find in Betyna one of the few examples of a truly caring spouse, she too must be hurt by her husband's aberrant, psychosexual problem, which is not entirely resolved even at the "happy" conclusion of this, one of the darkest, of Balabán's stories. And even the one pair of seemingly happy spouses, Timi's parents, as described by Gabriela in the story to which she lends her name, are shown in the concluding tale, "Ray Bradbury," to be far from marital bliss. They live separately, and a shocking divorce attempted through suicide has not yet been completely scarred over.

Love, and its failures, are more than a symptom of the disjointed modern world described by Balabán in his stories. Rather, he uses them, not unlike Oldřich's therapy, as a symbol for the cause of the disease: the rampant selfishness that sits at the root of societal atomisation. This is especially seen in the aforementioned "At the Communists," in which the sex act for Leoš is so auto-erotic in nature, that it can be replaced just as easily by onanism:

> *I c'n toss off at home under the covers on the airport even drunk. Three, four times a night, no problem. Of course, Leoš can do it, Leošek. Leoš, after Brezhnev, of course, Leonid! Not fucking Emperor Leopold, first or second! I don't have the good heart of an emperor. Don't have a good one, or a bad one. Don't have any at all.*

Whatever is eating him here — characteristically, he blames it on his mother — despite himself, he hits the nail on the head with the final diagnosis. He has no heart for anyone, save himself. And that can be said for more than a few of the contemporary Czechs that Balabán sets before us.

In this story, which describes as dysfunctional a family as one might ever find — a tyrannical woman who holds both son and husband under her thumb with a perverse dedication to casual sexual expression — it is not surprising that Leoš should find his perfect erotic match in an incestuous attraction to a newly discovered half-sister.

In Balabán's stories, sexual dysfunction and the eroding of the traditional significance of family can be seen as indicative of the breakdown of aimless contemporary society as a whole. In "Carousel Swings" the sensitive Hans reflects on this in a manner which repeats the auto-erotic metaphor of the runway-bed from Leoš's story:

> *To have children means the end of one's career. How stupid that sounds. Like from some idiotic soap opera retransmitted at three o'clock in the morning, when because of your insomnia you'll watch anything. Three years in the shithouse, and you'll fall out of everything. But not to have them, my God, and the whole world becomes an empty stomach, where there's room enough for everything, except a corner to snuggle in. One's bed is no longer a nest, but an airport, an international one at that, where*

each starts off from his own place in a different direction. Each unfaithful spouse with trembling knees thinks on that little piece of happiness... with someone else.

A strong, and palpable, current of Christian ethics pulses through the stories of Jan Balabán, who comes of the minority tradition of the Protestant Czech Brethren — his uncle Milan Balabán (born 1929) is an important theologian in the Protestant Reformed Church.[5] To what extent Balabán might be called a "Christian writer" as opposed to a "writer, who happens to be Christian" is difficult to assess. Petr Hruška is of the opinion that "his humble evangelical faith accompanies his sensitive reception of the ontological and existential frivolity of our murky lives."[6] Yet one needn't be a Christian to notice, as Mario Vargas Llosa does, that the emptying of the sexual act of any deeper significance in love, leads not only to its banalisation, but also the evaporation of its power to inform and positively aid in the construction of human society. In his criticism of Catherine Millet's autobiographical *La vie sexuelle de Catherine M.*, the Peruvian novelist writes:

> This book confirms what all the literature centred on sex has shown us, again and again. That, when sex is separated from the other activities and functions that constitute existence, it becomes extremely monotonic, with so limited a horizon that it eventually results in dehumanisation. A life defined (*imentada*) by sex, and only by sex, reduces this function to an organically primal activity, no more noble or pleasing than eating for the sake of eating or defecating. Only when it is civilised by culture and the charge of emotion and passion, and clothed (*reviste*) in ceremony and ritual, does sex enrich human life in an extraordinary way, its beneficent effects projecting themselves through all the paths and byways of existence.[7]

---

5 On the other end of the scale, so to speak, is the writer's brother, the accomplished Czech painter Daniel Balabán, who once attracted the criticism of Cardinal Miloslav Vlk for his admittedly heretical presentation of Jesus as a woman.

6 Hruška, p. 517.

7 Mario Vargas Llosa, *La civilización de espectáculo* (México: Punto de lectura, 2015), p. 127.

The characters that we find in the pages of this book exhibit a meagre aptitude for any sort of enrichment of life through sex, not to mention the giving sort of love, which is the only sort of real love. Each of them seem trapped in impermeable shells of self-interest, which make of matrimony a competition:

> Later, her accuracy in detecting his self-incrimination became unbearable. At times she even seemed inhuman. As if with that brilliance or cool elegance of hers she was one important step in front of him. At last he freed himself from his constricted horizons and began to comprehend that things were otherwise than had been pounded into his head since he was small. But she had known that already for a long time, and it was as if she had no patience for his belated discoveries. Back then he sincerely hoped that together, they could somehow overcome it all. Uršula also hoped that Roman would somehow grow out of it. But each of them hoped on their own, and thus they remained, even when their children came along.
> ("Ursula")

Even the best intentions of a married pair remain inert, if they are not revealed to the other person. Yet communication is a big problem for the married pairs in the pages of Balabán's work, who, even when they desire contact, shrink back from it at the last moment, as if they were afraid of losing something through this cession of autonomy:

> And third, Hans certainly didn't imagine that the dog understood him, and so he was actually talking to himself. In his metaphors and parables he's vainly searching for a narrow passage between his Scylla — the faithful dog — and Charybdis — the wild wolf — only to discover with horror, that no such passage exists. *You can be this, Hans, or that. You can envy the dog his master, or the wolf his freedom. Oh, how well do I know that!* Anna Marie whispered to herself standing there with her ear close to the foyer door, while being at the same time as far from there as the moon is above the mountains.
> Her fingers were already near the handle, so as to bring this moment with Hans/without Hans to a conclusion, when she

backed away from the door on tiptoe. She wasn't a fan of sudden sentimental embraces, and everything seemed to be heading that way at the moment.

As one can see from the above-cited fragment from "His Master's Voice," it's not that Balabán's creations lack the reflective quality which, according to the philosophers, makes life worth living. But there is a second step, and that one is outward, toward the other person. And it is this that sours nearly all of the relationships one finds in the pages of *Maybe We're Leaving*. The interactions of husband and wife in Balabán's stories are full of missed opportunities, as in this excerpt from "Pyrrhula Pyrrhula:"

> After a moment, both of them met at the summit of the sharp ridge, which divided one abyss from the other. The brisk wind clung to their sweating skin. They seemed to be naked; like some kind of creatures other than people, when they embraced, resting chest upon chest, and breathing heavily past the other's shoulder. Michal felt Věra's heart beating, as if he didn't have one of his own.
> Then they retreated to a little sheltered depression overgrown with dwarf pine and alders. They drank some water and ate their bread and cheese. Michal stretched out on his back and gazed up at the sky which, from the east was burdening over with dark clouds, which disturbed the heretofore sunny weather. *Just a bit, and we'll be chattering our teeth in mist and downpour. Just a bit, and we'll be screaming words of reproach at one another, our eyes bulging in fury.*

But why? One wishes to scream at him, at this moment. Why must it end in a quarrel? In Balabán's stories, it seems as if discord is the natural environment of male-female relationships, and every respite therefrom is fleeting at best. "*Bednář, Alice, the things they say about you both!*" reflects Hans, the outsider in his friends' apartment, as he sits there dumbfounded at how it can be, that a lucky man like Bednář simply can't grasp the great good fortune he has in a wife such as Alice:

> *If even only half of it were true, you'd already have been done to death. And you, Alice, set a tray with splendid sandwiches on the*

table all the same and I stuff myself with them, as if I hadn't eaten for a fortnight, and I drink the wine over which you were just shedding tears in the kitchen. Carefully, I praise Bednář's pictures and meanwhile, mostly, I study your eyes to see that you're not pained by it. I look at Bednář and wonder if he senses it; and the only thing I sense myself is that you're both happy I'm here, because you won't quarrel until I leave.

Now, Jan Balabán's world is a fallen one, a faulty one, and perhaps a rather unpleasant one. But as every reader of *The Waste Land* knows, Eliot doesn't just show us the arid desert of post World War I Europe, he also shows us a way out of it. Similarly, Balabán is neither nihilist nor especially pessimist. Even his most broken characters, as we have noted, are not victims. For all the Calvinism which may inform his Protestant tradition, he is no fatalist, and his characters are neither passive robots nor helpless spiders in the hands of an angry God. The way out is an acceptance of responsibility, for one, and for those one loves, even — perhaps especially — in the most difficult circumstances. This is seen in the devotion shown by Vladimír to Edita when, after so much hatred and anger, he still gets out of bed and drives across town to bring her "home" after she is abandoned by the man she left him for, and even though he knows that the cycle of bitterness and anger will begin again next morning:

> Vladimír cruised about the streets, rather than heading straight home. They had time enough. That's one thing they had. He drove out onto the beltway and circled the city in a wide arc many kilometres long. On purpose, he drew out the ride through the peripheral suburbs and the nearby villages, where not a single light was shining in any of the cottages. He wanted to remember this moment, driving about like that all night long, because in the morning, in the morning everything would be quite different.

It is seen in the dedication of Betyna to her sick husband Oldřich, patiently bearing with his incapacities, shouldering the responsibilities of the household, and pressuring him to seek a cure for his phobias, remaining with him even after the hurtful episode during which he blames her, and their unborn child, for his troubles. The head physician in "The Cedar and the Hammer" puts it plainly in her conversation with Dr Kraus, a biologist at the same hospital, undergoing his second rehab for an alcoholism fed by despair and (it seems) self-pity:

> — *You know, a person needs a solution* [says Kraus]. *He needs someone to be with, in good and in bad. Especially in the bad, you know, when everyone stands there looking at you as if you were a dead cow.*
> — *I understand you quite well, Mr Kraus. But you also need to understand that a person needs to accept responsibility for his own actions, and not just wait for other people to help.*

Jan Balabán's world — and is it not the world we all inhabit? — is far from perfect. But it is not escape from that world that we need, but acceptance of its, and our, limitations, and engagement with it, with other people, in kindness and understanding. This is what prompts Hans' meditations in the attic of the rectory where his grandfather was pastor years before:

> The vicarage attic was a perfect pyramid raised on a square base of sturdy beams. When he was a child, the deep, longitudinal cracks in the beams frightened Hans with the thought that the roof might cave in. Later, when he came to realise that all beams are cracked, this became the basis of his attitude toward life. After the disillusionments that resulted from his yearning toward perfection, he formulated the rule that, if he must be fragile, at least he will be fragile in a good way.
> ("Diana")

It is noteworthy that Karel Chudoba, the physician-grandfather of "Ray Bradbury," who is nearing the end of his road, gasping into brief consciousness every day against the tide of Alzheimer's, delivers one of the most hopeful messages in the book. We must continue to strive; we must continue to strive to do good. He may, when the disease knocks him out, allow his grandson Timoteus to lead him to bed like "an obedient robot," but when conscious, he fights on to the end. Even if he can't recognise quite who he is talking to, he still has a message to deliver:

"You know, my boy, a person has to return to where he belongs. Home. Even if that home isn't a welcoming one. And even if you had to return only to accept punishment, you've got to return. That punishment is part of your life, too."

"But we are home," Tim replied.

"No, we don't belong here. We have to return home. Even before they send us there in a sealed casket or a plastic bag, boy."

[...]

"It's a kind of paradox, son," Chudoba calmed his supposed son with a quick gesture of his hand. "I can quite clearly see the edges of my blindness. I know for sure that I will cease to know. But that's all right — it can happen to anyone. God allows it. But do you know what God does not forgive?"

Again that smile of false teeth between skewed lips.

"God does not forgive those who escape. And I must stop escaping; I must go there."

In this collection of interweaving narratives, linked by the appearance of characters in multiple stories, Timoteus, the doctor's grandson, and Gabriela, the girlfriend whom he had to put off meeting in order to "take care of Gramps," provide us with a subtle, visible example of right action — and the recognition thereof. Although raised in a godless household, in the orbit of a grandfather no less troubled and perverse than Leoš's mother, it is Gábi who visits the old man's grave each month, tidying it, and even lighting a votive candle near the old Communist's headstone. "She visited the grave like clockwork, on foot or on her bike [...] and would have done, as her grandfather might have said, even if it were raining hatchets." There is no easy explanation for why she does this, since, unlike Timoteus, she was not raised in a Christian home and is, at best, an agnostic in reference to the possibility of an afterlife.[8] Still, whether or not we intuitively perform right actions like the agnostic Gabriela, we should at least be as open to the world and actively engaged with it as the Christian Timoteus, to learn from the actions of others, and better ourselves, and the world, by imitating them:

---

8   Even if, as the author suggests, Gabriela feels "cleansed" after performing this ritual, the question remains: cleansed of what? If this is an act of penitence, then, penitence on behalf of whom?

> Timoteus was sitting on the edge of a neighbouring grave,
> lost in thought and breathless. Even though he wasn't doing
> anything, it seemed to him that he was witnessing something
> spiritual. On the graves round about there were angels, in stone
> and plaster — only above the grave of old Čestmír and his poor
> wife there hovered a real angel — and to top it all off, Gabriel.
> ("Gabriela")

Sure, to our ears this sounds almost too cute. But what should we
expect, alumni of such a cynical, sarcastic, and snarky society as
our own? Balabán is too good a writer to fall into kitsch. If the
story ends on a supposedly saccharine note, we can be sure that
it was so calculated by the author. He doesn't care about our wry
smiles at Timoteus' sudden enlightenment, or the way he expresses
it. This too is an example of Balabán's aesthetic of hyper-realism,
for at times, the spiritual *will* emerge from all the gritty sand and
filth of this dead world, "shining out, like shook foil," as Gerard
Manley Hopkins put it amidst the industrial squalor of brick-skirted
nineteenth century England, with whom Balabán may have been
familiar from the splendid Czech translations of Rio Preisner and
Ivan Slavík. What is important here is the effect this has on the
seemingly passive beholder, Timi. He, who had longed to have sex
with Gabriela rebelliously, right at the cemetery gates, no longer sees
her as merely an object of desire. She becomes a woman here in this
angelic transformation through service, and his lust is sublimated
into love, if it had not been so already. He no longer wishes to judge
her, shocked as he was that she would visit consecrated ground in
shorts and a bikini top: it is a transfigurative, Tabor moment, and he
sees her clothed in light.

In both stories in which they appear, Gabriela and Timoteus are
presented as sympathetic, likeable characters. They are young, and
their whole life is ahead of them. The cynic in us wishes to smirk:
Sure, at eighteen, everybody's an idealist; everybody who's in love at
that age has found his soul mate. As Morrissey sings, "Hand in glove, /
the sun shines out of our behinds. / No, it's not like any other love, / this
one is different, because it's us." Let's see them when they are forty,
and throwing dishes at one another in front of the kids. But actually
this has nothing to do with experience or immaturity, youth or age.

It all has to do with the will to sympathise, the will to love. In "Pyrrhula Pyrrhula," the vicious outbreak that Michal is sure is coming doesn't arrive after all. The last image we have of him and his wife is during their descent through the mountainous terrain of Slovakia on the ski-lift, with Věra's head nestled against her husband's shoulder as he drones on, lulling her to sleep. Even before that, at the summit of the mountain, there occurs this striking scene:

> Mist was rising up from the valley to the right. It didn't flop over the ridge onto the valley on the left, but rose straight up, as if obeying an invisible partition that divided the space. The valley on the right was full of mist, while that on the left was clean and deep, with those touching little houses and cottages and flocks of sheep at the foothills. And at the borderline of the clearly seen world and that other, suspected one, where the clouds met with the bright current of sunrays, two figures in windbreakers were moving along, one behind the other, yet holding hands, as if one were leading the other.

The image of these two people, silhouetted against the sky, walking along hand in hand, cannot but call to mind the final scene of Bergman's masterpiece, *The Seventh Seal.* There, in a contemporary film that almost tortures the spectator with its wrenching questions concerning faith, the sense of life, and the existence of God in a world that had just undergone the Hell of the Second World War, we are treated to a composition straight out of the Middle Ages, the Ages of Faith: Death leads a string of people of both sexes and all states of life, dancing along an upland ridge, *upwards.* It is a subtle scene, but one that is difficult to interpret in a negative way. For we behold this harvest of Death through the eyes of the itinerant actor and mystic Jof, who earlier on beheld a vision of the Virgin Mary and the Child Jesus. It is an image of hope, right where one would least expect to find it.

Similarly, in the Christmas tale "Bethesda," the musician/theology student become cynical number-cruncher Ludvík experiences a revelation of his own. Sitting in a bar, overhearing the hard life story of the shabby CD huckster he had earlier chased out of his office, his better nature awakens:

Sir, I have no man. And what did Jesus say to that? Ludvík felt himself flush with heat, and his hands grow terribly weak. *What did he say? Arise and walk! Twenty forty — sixty eighty — one hundred one hundred twenty — one hundred forty one hundred sixty — how much you got on you?*

But just as he is about to approach the man and buy the entire box of kitschy music in an uprush of practical charity, the man exits the bar, and the moment passes. An opportunity to make a difference passes away too, and all we are left with is one man's good intentions — which can feed no one. So, certainly, hope for a better world, and better people, is not missing from the stories that make up Balabán's book. But that hope can only be brought to fruition by our determined, positive actions. "Hurry up please, it's time," calls the apocalyptic barman in Eliot's pub. That call echoes to us, through the short stories of Jan Balabán too, with no less urgency. Because the moment passes by so very quickly.

Alexandria, Virginia
16 September 2017

EMIL

Ah, you OpenLates, you NonStops, pawnshops and casinos! Ah, you…! The fascists should shut you all down. And by that I don't mean white *skinned* fascists, but fascists *in white*, even coloured fascists, fascist angels, fascist doctors, sisters and brothers in white coats with white belts and white manacles. When will they be called, at last, to the vanguard of the state to protect us from this filth, this sludge through which we wade from pawnshop to NonStop? Where are you sleeping, you white knights, as we are left behind here, at the mercy of the open shops of those usurious vermin?

Back then under the Commies one could only drink until ten o'clock, to midnight at the latest, and you could buy yourself a bottle until nine o'clock only, and that perhaps at only two places in the whole town. That's the reason I bought my safety light. A beautiful ten-litre bottle with a grounded stopper. And my brother, that great and strong man, who always taught me things that destroyed me but were unable to harm him, my brother helped me to fill it with ten thousand grammes of one-hundred percent spirit.

My brother was an operational engineer in a perfume factory. As such, he could get his hands on as much pure alcoholic spirits as he wished, and yet he never tested his liver. He mixed splendid cocktails from essence with which to tempt the laboratory girls. Then he drove them to the shack in his car, and later he'd tell me all about their tight squeezes, their nipples and their dexterous lips. Meanwhile I was always left with my head resting on the table before the fun even began. And then those long, unbearable nights, when I oscillated from the closed doors of stores and stands to the train station until morning without the slightest glimmer of even the worst sort of firewater. Breathless, swigless, in a night as dark as the grave. For this very reason my brother obtained that lantern for me, whose light would see me through to the end of the very longest night.

Half dead, I dragged it up to the cabinet in my wretched room. I set it on the altar, after which, exhausted, I fell down onto my unmade bed and from there I gazed upon it with the certainty that never again would I find myself alone in my shivering, goose-bumped skin. And it was exactly then that freedom came, and the doors of the stores and pawnshops opened wide, never to close again.

At that moment, my holy tabernacle seemed to lose its worth. I never reached for it again. From then on I always bought a case, or hip-flask, or a plastic vessel with something thinner and cloudier. From then on I guzzled myself to sleep with a mundane stream of something like that. No more could I cast my eyes upon the transparent brightness of pure light. I turned my gaze away from it, and allowed dust to settle on the lamp.

"There's still time." The sulphurous yellow numbers on the alarm clock showed 4:10. "There's still time!"

Emil grew calm at the idea that he didn't have to get up for at least three more hours. Didn't even have to budge. Yet the margins of that prospect were sullied by the thought that it all begins in two hours. The sounds of the street would begin. The lorries would begin to rumble out of the warehouses. The trams would roll away like children's trains when the batteries are engaged. The dustmen would begin their banging beneath the windows. And the sounds of the house would start. People would start to move about on the other side of the walls, flushing toilets, filling bathtubs and turning on showers. Steps on the stairs. *Ah*. He pulled the cover up to his chin.

The sounds of the flat would begin. The dog would scratch at the door, demanding a walk. The children's bed would creak, his wife, motionless on the mattress beside him, would move… *No she wouldn't!* On faith, he reached out for her; she was not there.

This happened from time to time. He would forget where he was and what was going on with him. No, it wasn't a matter of memory, but conversely, of intensive recollection. The signs are just too deeply cut in the soft structure of memory, and they come to life, even though they may have been deprived of the rights of domicile, long ago. They arise of their own accord and Emil, like it or not, would remember his family without consciously trying to, while at the same time he'd have to expend great effort to remember last night, how it came to be that again he was lying there like a cold fish on a pan. It was like working at a terribly irritating crossword, the answers of which he already knew, and now, just for the sake of order, he was to fill in all of those horizontals and verticals, so to make sense out of it all.

Senseless! He must defend himself from this, and his only defence is sleep. There is time enough. I force him to. After all, I am the writer of the script, the director of these images. I am the dream factory.

I start up my old car. The only car I trust. It's quite unsightly. The paint has disappeared beneath patches of automobile primer. Inside, everything is decrepit and sagging, but the tires, the tires have a deep tread and the chassis is treated with an asphalt coating, all pins and hinges covered with grease. That's important. In this aggressive environment you've got to cover the cooler grid with a fatty vellum and conserve all uncovered parts from the salts in the air. My car will never be eaten by rust.

The lights of the last village grow smaller in the rear view mirror. I'm driving through a dark forest of fir. Looking up I see the edge of the indigo blue heavens where they meet the black, ragged fringe of the summits of the conifers. I emerge at the summit of the forest, where the firs bend and kneel like stunted bushes lashed by the wind from the sea. Further on, only the cape stretches out its rocky back, and at its steep end over the dark restless mass of the sea a lighthouse, on the top of which shines the bright light of the lamp I tend.

I stop here. I get out of the car, my lungs unable to bear the sharp gusts of wind. Behind the doors of the garage I light a cigarette. I drive the car inside and cover it with a wax-covered tarp. I tug the wings of the doors against the wind. At last I push fast the pin. I look at my watch: it's four ten. There's still time. I hear the mechanism of the lighthouse working in the wind. I go up to the stone parapet at the edge of the reef. On the backs of the black waves the grey mould of the nearing dawn appears. The beating waves strike the chalky reef and hiss, as if it were not made of limestone, but of quicklime. They scratch at the reef, which does not diminish.

I raise my eyes and find the light of the lamp on the opposite side. I just imagine the little houses asleep like a flock of sheep huddled up for the night. From them to the sea runs the long, very long concrete pier and, at its end, the striped steel chimney of the second tower, with its lamp at the top. When the ship's pilot sees both of our lights aligned, he can steer his keel safely over the rocks until he catches sight of the third lantern on the cape, hidden past the slope of the mountain.

The night is bright; the foghorn doesn't need to be sounded, which otherwise above my cosy apartment at the foot of the lighthouse would groan like a wounded animal stuck on the reef. Today I can sit at my cup of tea in peace, waiting for the arrival of the first birds, just like every day. That's why I'm here: to sit with my strongly sweetened tea, looking out to sea and watching for the birds. I'm writing a book about them. This is my tenth year spent at the rookeries. The tenth year I keep my lamp full, writing letters to my wife, who also busies herself with seabirds. She is as beautiful as an auk, a gannet, and her letters fold like the wings of an albatross.

In the morning, when the tide is out, I step down to the beach. The sky is covered. From the high clouds a small rain is falling on the sand packed tight and flat as a board by the waves. Out on the waves a boat appears. It is a fast, modern motorboat. In it there is one figure, that of a man, a sailor. I've never seen him and never will, because no boat can land here without wrecking. Wave and call all you want, signal until your arms fall off, you simply can't reach my shore. From that direction nobody can come to me, except the birds.

Emil woke up for the second time. He got out of bed, opened the window, and set the coffee on. He turned on the stream of hot water above him in the shower, to wash away the sweat of the night. Then, with his coffee and in a clean shirt he called his girlfriend at work.

"How was your shift?"

"Didn't get much sleep. There was an emergency."

"What time?"

"A little after four."

"That's curious."

"What's curious about it?"

"Nothing. Did he die?"

"No. Not yet. He's in intensive care."

On the way to work he stopped at the corner store. It was open all night. In the morning, the shopgirls had had quite enough of that. Two scruffy types at the counter were packing boxes of cheap wine into a large, grubby bag.

"One more," grumbled the one who looked like the older of the two brothers, "we have enough for one more," and he scattered the last of their coins on the counter. Both were hardly able to stand on their legs. Emil waited until his turn came. He glanced their way and said to himself, *Too little, way too little, boys!* And thought of those ten thousand pellucid grammes.

DIANA

Hans parked on the village green below the vicarage. The large building looked out from between the green crowns of the trees like a familiar, pale, flushed face. *Only in a country where the air is free of dust particles, and the rain is not polluted or acidic, can plaster age like that. A country, where one only washes the windows before the holidays, and more for the sake of the holidays than because they need a washing.* He slammed the car door and squeamishly touched the windscreen, covered in crushed bugs. He pressed down with his index finger until the nail turned white, and made a vertical line through that bloody gunk beyond the reach of the wipers. It could have been an *i*, or the first stroke of another letter. *Everything begins with a vertical line, after all, and those letters that don't contain a vertical, are at least symmetrical to it.* He abandoned his letter and set off toward the house, in which his grandfather, the pastor, once lived. When he was a child, he always liked the way the house turned an amiable countenance toward the countryside. Today, of course, the look of its deep, curtainless windows seemed tragic, rather; dark, like the eyes of a lunatic.

Beneath the tree before the entrance to the house all was abustle. A large commercial auto stood there. A Volvo, or a Mercedes. It was a Mercedes, but from the very first Hans felt the need to call it a Volvo, and so it remained. The young rector, along with a few helpers, was filling the van with furniture, the contents of the entire household: computers and televisions in their original boxes. The rector's wife, a small, somewhat rounded person, with her thick hair pulled up in a tight bun, was leaning against the granite door frame, a cigarette trembling between her fingers. Despite himself, Hans noticed the nervous movement with which she flicked the non-existent ash from its tip. Among all this bustle of moving the broad-shouldered and mustached servant of God seemed somehow calm, in control, and Hans guessed that this move was more his idea than hers.

"Ah, hello. I suppose you've come for those books of your grandfather's. They're upstairs in the attic. We left them in the chest where they were when we moved in. You know, at first I had some ideas for that attic. I wanted to rearrange it and put in some skylights. It would have made a fine studio, and Marta paints a little bit…"

Hans called to mind some New Year's cards with vegetation, motifs of thorns and rose-hips wound about chalice and cross. Drab and cloying…. *Kitsch*, said Hans' brother, a painter, cutting off all further discussion.

"…but that was beyond our means. Especially considering the straitened circumstances of a rector's life, as you well know. So in short we left it alone. Except for the addition of a few of our old things tossed in up there. I didn't venture up there often, but I guess there are a few things left behind from each rector. And we won't be any different. If I had to take everything with me, I'd bust. You know, moving is worse than…"

Hans disdained the obligatory allusion to conflagration, and instead of that tossed out something acerbic in the style of "the Lord God will dispose of this junk of ours in His own time."

"You're absolutely right," sighed the rector sympathetically, breathing hard.

He grew quiet for the first time since Hans' arrival, and trained his eyes on his spouse, standing indecisively in the doorframe. The half-filled interior of the Volvo behind him lent it something of the dull appearance of a modern church.

"There are some other of your grandfather's books in the cabinet so to speak, behind the chimney. Marta will show you where, but…" he laughed, "you know the place, after all, and we, we really don't live here any more."

Yet all the same Marta took the trouble to lead him past the doorways of the abandoned bedrooms and empty study, to the stairs leading to the attic.

"You know, we lived here for seven years," she said to him softly, "but we never really got used to it. These country people are odd, but all the same," she said, nodding her head, as if she were agreeing with someone, "all the same, I'll miss it all." She smiled shyly.

The vicarage attic was a perfect pyramid raised on a square base of sturdy beams. When he was a chili, the deep longitudinal cracks in the beams frightened Hans with the thought that the roof might cave in. Later, when he came to realise that all beams are cracked, this became the basis of his attitude toward life. After the disillusionments that resulted from his yearning toward perfection, he formulated the rule that, if he must be fragile, at least he will be fragile in a good way.

The spot beneath the apex of the roof was fixed to the chimney with what is known as a chimney bridge. From that bridge, Hans and his brother and cousins from the numerous clan would throw themselves onto a pile of mattresses stacked on conjugal beds retired from service. They called this a "buck jump," according to the logic of a vulgar boy's joke, which gave them to understand that in this way, more or less, they would one day jump on women.

There were bucks here as well. Here and there, on a cabinet, on a chest, dully shining porcelain bucks, bucks surrounded by wolves, a buck and a doe looking about a glade, a buck leaping. On the laminated marble top of an old table there was a whole herd of them. His grandfather the rector would get them from the country people as a confirmation gift — that is, for the labour of catechesis, testing, and performing the ceremony by which young Protestants were initiated to the Lord's Table, and to full communion with the congregation of their brothers and sisters in the Lord. The great number of the porcelain herd testified to the many generations that Grandpa had led into the Church. *But that herd was left without a shepherd. Deer don't need a shepherd, though. Mere symbols,* Hans thought.

Behind the chimney stood a cabinet indeed, stained at one time with a reddish lacquer. His grandfather's library had already been properly picked through, yet he still found a pile of books that drew him close to that man, as peculiar as the country people, and yet a pastor, to whom even the educated gave heed. Little by little he set aside Jan Blahoslav Čapek's *Ardour of the Spirit*, Milíč Lochman's *Czech Rebirth*, T.G. Masayrk's *Czech Question* and *Suicide*, Herben's *The Poor Boy who Became Famous*, a *Grand Illustrated Atlas of Animals*, Slavomil Daňek's *Historical Background to the Old Testament*, Brehm's *Life of the Animals*, Amicise's *The Heart*, and Chelčicky's *Net of Faith*. So many other books, the spines of which he stroked with his eyes as they rested behind the panes of the library bookshelves during evening prayers, were now gone. He made a little column of the books he had extracted, and then he returned one or two to the shelves, so that there'd still be something left for others.

From the floors below him he heard the rumble of furniture being dragged. For a moment he seemed to be in a ship, where the sailors were rolling barrels about below deck. Just like in childhood, when he would lay on those old beds up here with his cousin, reading Kipling's *Captains Courageous* before falling asleep. As if they were in a ship's cabin. And there was a sort of cabin up here: a cabin of planks fixed between the beams, a little dark-room covered on the outside with the black papers from boxes of film. They called it the dungeon. That's where photos were developed. First by Grandad, then the uncles took over, and finally they themselves, fifteen-year-old boys. In the red light they bathed the paper in developing fluid, and watched as the image began to appear. "Everything's born from a slit," his cousin always used to say, alluding to juvenile dirty joke. *True right, everything's born from a slit,* he thought, *regardless of sex and wombs. Even a door starts off as a slit, before it becomes a rectangle.* He threw a glance inside. It was as empty as the Holy of Holies. And then he suddenly remembered Diana. *She ought to be around here somewhere.* He searched for her in the rear, in the dust, beneath the very bevel of the roof, where they used to toss her.

The memory came as bright as a flash of lightning. He set his hand down on a roll of dust-covered wrapping paper. When he unrolled it in the bright square of the skylight, a large pencil drawing of a female nude met his eyes. At the feet of the naked woman was written: *Great is Diana of the Ephesians.* That was what the pagans in Ephesus shouted at the apostle Paul, when he preached the Gospel to them; and this is what Hans' brother drew one evening after Bible Hour, in the attic by flashlight, on the floor, with the breathless assistance of the rest of the old pastor's grandchildren. She had large breasts, hefty hips and an uncovered lap. She looked like Ornella Mutti in the film *First Love.*

Hans chuckled. Despite all of her seductiveness and the emphasised attributes of her femininity, this Diana looked more like a boy — a terrified boy in a woman's body. All studies of the female anatomy were still far in Hans' brother's future — and not his alone — and the artists were still unable to help their drawings along with photos. *These days, it's only photographs for most people. But this Diana here, well, she's a proper one.* Hans let go of the top edge and Diana once again curled up into a tube. He wanted to take her with him, *but what for, really?* He took the roll of paper and tossed it behind the cabinet again, into its place in the corner.

He picked up the column of books and, suddenly didn't have enough. He spun about with the books in his arms in the cone of light, out of breath, emotional. And then, so as to fix the moment, he set on top a couple of the deer — those escaping, with wounded legs.

The pastor's wife laughed, amused to see him come down the stairs, all grubby with dust, clutching the books and the deer in his arms.

"Those beasts, eh?" She chirped. "Me and Petr were always wondering how they got there in the first place."

"Oh, it's a long story. And you're in a hurry," said Hans by way of excuse.

"Well, come along and wash up, at least. Except there's no towels there now."

Hans dried his hands, more or less, on his pants legs, bid the couple farewell, and moved off to the trees on the village green. He noticed that the large Volvo was now almost full — such as contemporary churches never are. Soon the pastor and his wife would be off, and the vicarage would be orphaned. They call it an unstaffed parish.

The slit-like line he drew was still in its place on the upper windscreen. He placed the books in the boot and the deer on the seat.

"I'll take you next time, Diana," he said in a quiet voice, and turned the key in the ignition.

MAGDA

Jaromír went further today than he had ever gone before. Quietly, he disappeared from his home street, made up of six identical houses on each side. The pea-green stucco, which clung to the thick surface of the panels like a frog, distinguished it from the neighbouring streets, where the identical walls dripped a reddish-grey colour, as if the houses were bleeding through their chinks. Jaromír ran through the foreign, inimical courtyards of houses of different hues, all of which would pale completely, growing similar to one another, when that twelve-year-old boy would become a grown man rushing, day after day, through the colourless morning to the bus, and it would never occur to him that once these houses had their own tones of colour.

There will remain only shades, fixed, precisely defined rectangles dropped onto the splitting asphalt of the streets, which over the years groups of asphalters would patch and patch until you wouldn't be able to tell, which is the patch, and which is the original road surface. *And so it is with this life, which year after year can't afford a new coat.* For the moment safely distanced from adulthood, Jaromír walked along the outlying streets, covered in mud. The mud was compressed by the tyres of commercial trucks into strange ridges and crests, formed by their patterns. As he crossed over them carefully, they seemed to be of iron, like the discarded treads of tanks. Past them, the path led through piles of yellow clay surmounting deep pits, in which workers were setting the framework for concrete pours. Jaromír picked his way, silently, beneath the branches of rowan, around stakes with signs reading *Keep Out,*[9] which one understood differently back

---

9 *Nezaměstnaným vstup zakázán,* which literally means: "Access forbidden to the unemployed." In the Communist years, everyone was theoretically employed, so the signs meant "if you don't work here, keep out." However, the paranoia of Communist régimes in East-Central Europe set up such signs, including "Photographing Prohibited" in the most incongruous places. The

then, and he stood there gazing at the fearfully tanned bodies of the workers, at their muscles, their chests and stomachs, and listening to those horrid words that flew out of their mouths. *That was a piece of work.* Mama said that they were criminals working there, prisoners, but he saw no chains nor guards with rifles. *Who knows what their story really was.*

He made his way around the pits, passing fenced-in lots with building material and the whole background works of a construction site, and suddenly, he found himself in the fields. The firm surface of the road changed into a footpath, which ran on and on among fields of maize. In the distance, beyond the limitless space of the fields, rose up the wet summits of real mountains, which Jaromír was to visit in the future, after he had joined a scout troop. In the meanwhile, they were just unknown, distant mountains, and the fields of maize extended beneath them like a savannah.

Jaromír suddenly felt that he needed to go number two. He was so far away from everything. But the maize fields with its plants, taller than he, burgeoning in their leafy furrows, also seemed inaccessible. How could he get in among them without getting caught up there, and how was he supposed to pull down his pants in that thicket? So he preferred to squat down on his heels. They called that the Indian Plug. Indeed, after a bit the urge passed, and Jaromír went on.

Now he was really far away. The houses and the construction site disappeared beyond the maize. The footpath ran past a strange building, to which he never gave much thought. The bulging walls in the clasp of iron traverse beams threatened collapse, and those great arches over the doors that stretched the length of the front wall… a, *hangar…* tumbled through his head, as he pressed on at a quicker pace. *And if there were still airplanes inside? Airplanes with machine guns from the Second World War.* Daddy once told him that there was an airport somewheres hereabout, where the pilots would drop mail pouches. Already only the arches could be seen above the maize. He pressed on for that very reason, so as not to have to return. He kept looking around him anxiously, and when at last he looked well to the front, he stopped dead in his tracks, and his mouth hung open.

---

reference may be a political one; obviously, in the post-Communist period, the unemployed may be seen as undesirable for other reasons.

For it was then that he saw the giant oaks. Extraordinarily strong and twisted branches lifted up to the sky their crowns of sharp green leaves. It was a grand oasis — a large clump of oaks[10] in the midst of the fields, fitted about with smaller shrubs of birch and hornbeam. The path narrowed into a tight passage, almost a tunnel, where branches lashed his face and nettles left their burning traces on his bare knees and calves. He squeezed through all of this tightness and, excited with a fear that he had just barely overcome, he entered the deep shade at the foot of the trees. Dried leaves and acorns rustled and crackled beneath his feet, but Jaromír had no eyes for them. He stood there with his head bent backwards, gazing up at the living vault of the glade, which he named at this moment — *Dubovina. Yes, Dubovina, Dubovina!*[11] This was for him alone — no one else knew anything about it — about that shade stretching up to the heavens, about those trunks as massive as the piers of a church.

No one had been here for many years. Over here were the traces of a long-doused campfire, over there… A gnarled vine was hanging between two trees, a strong, twisted withe from long ago. It took him a while to realise that it was a swing. He sat on the twist, held it with both his hands, and began to swing back and forth slowly. Then he lifted up his legs and rose into the air like a bird. He swung back and forth, again and again, kicking off always at the lowest point. Quite alone, he did things here, which he never before would have dared.

I won't tell a soul. I'll keep it dark from everybody. Soon his house arose before him again. The whole family was in the kitchen. His father was getting ready for the night shift, his brothers and sisters were babbling confusedly, trying to outshout the others and he, Mirek, Jaromírek, sat down over his homework and entered a chronicle of his Dubovina into his notebook. He remained there among the circle of trees, where a stream of light fell through the gap between the crowns, and listened. He listened quietly to his breathing, to his voice, singing the suddenly discovered, new hymn.

---

10   In Czech: *Byla to veliká remíza, spíš jakýsi remíz dubů.* The sentence contains a play on words which is untranslatable in English: Balabán glances *remíz* (clump, copse, hammock) off *remíza* (wayside inn, rest-stop).

11   *Dub* = oak. The proper name he gives the place, *Dubovina*, means something like Oak-glade, Oak-land.

Magda felt like she couldn't breathe. And yet there was quite enough space here — just the bare walls and those few things gathered together of a sudden: those indispensables you grab at the moment of need. She couldn't catch her breath. Tomorrow they'll bring the child, and the crib, some furniture. *I've got no chandelier.* She looked at the two wires hanging from hooks in the ceiling. *But I'd rather not turn on a light here anyway. The little lamp near the mattress on the floor will suffice. And paint. I have to paint. Dear God, I won't survive this.* She gasped for breath like a fish.

She opened the doors giving on to the balcony and stood there on the threshold. The grating made her halt. Not that of the doors, but the grating, which closed off the area of the balcony. Rusty iron bars welded to the original railing and somehow set into the edge of the ceiling, or rather the floor of the balcony above, on the first storey. *I knew it was going to be on the ground-floor, but… like this?* The lower edge of the balcony was no higher than some hundred and twenty centimetres above *how should I say it… the surrounding terrain.* Thus Magda found a fitting word for the footworn yard and pavement, the cobbles of which, obviously, had been set directly into the muddy earth, and were cocked at crazy angles, some wrenched up entirely, on all sides. A well-worn path that ran beside the pavement, and the ruts made by children's bikes, testified to the fact that the pavement itself was unfit for walking on. *And when it rains — what a swine! What a proper swine, that architect, to design and build a house with a balcony only a hundred and twenty centimetres above the ground — an invitation to burglars! The brute, who knew that he would never be living in these houses raised up in the old maize fields. "Let'm bar themselves in, the proles," he says, strutting up the lawn toward his villa, which he raised with the money that everybody around here lacks. Does he? Ha, he doesn't say a thing. Doesn't waste a second thought on the proles.*[12]

And so they bar themselves in. I can see the chaps at the grind with their welding tools and bottles. Iron bars. Home sweet home behind bars. But there's just one problem. When you've barred up the balcony on the ground floor, you've made a pretty ladder to the balcony on the first floor. And so they weld some bars one floor higher. But now the neighbour on the second floor starts to get nervous. For sure you'll find a climber who'll

---

12   The word that Balabán uses here is a bit stronger: *otroci* = slaves.

climb up over the bars and onto the second floor. And so the bars grow a floor higher, to the third storey… Now that burglar'd have to be Zorro the Avenger himself, but, who knows? Where lies the border between nerve and anxiety? Sometimes even the third storey balconies are barred, to the sadness and anger of the fourth, but usually they stop at the second. And so houses cover themselves with bars and become cloisters of a sort. But thank God for the bars, Magda thought, *that's all I need, for somebody to come crawling in here over the balcony.*

Not made up, in a tight white t-shirt, her hair short and reddish, in red capris, with the cement floor beneath her bare feet, she breathes the barred-in air and trembles like a mare. Somewhere on the floor above her, an automatic washing machine on the spin cycle is thumping against the wall. Thumping and endlessly thumping. *Some people. Ah!* Magda sits down on the plastic chair left behind by the previous tenant. She lights a cigarette and balls herself up into the intimate area bordered by her shoulders and knees, collarbones, small breasts, lap and arms. *Here I'm home. Here I'll make your crib, little boy.* She smokes and sobs a little bit. *We'll go to the discount store in the old hangar together, shopping. You'll like the arches. And on our walks we'll make a little detour into that little wood of oaks, all shattered and bruised, left among the prefabs. There nobody'll find us.*

BETHESDA

When Ludvík saw the man for the first time, he didn't really notice him at all. It was a pedlar who simply knocked at the door of his office, hawking CDs with popular music. Collections of classic hits.

"You don't have any classical music?" asked Ludvík, who simply loathed collections of hits, especially *for Christmas, as presents...*

"Classical music, classical music..." mumbled the pedlar blushing. "I've got some orchestral arrangements... Different old standards and evergreens arranged for orchestra... mood music to listen to and relax."

"No, that's not going to work," replied Ludvík, walking the pedlar to the door.

He sat back down at his computer. But before he got back to work, he thought a moment more about that man, whose face he already couldn't recall. Where did he come from? *I guess he's just trying his luck.* The doorman was just about to eject him along with those orchestral arrangements of his.

Gazing at his monitor, Ludvík didn't notice that the rain outside the window had begun to bloom with sparse flakes of snow. Once he had studied music, then even theology — he had this twisted period in his life, when he wanted to "serve" — and in the end, he finished in this well-paying, but gruelling grind at the computer. At work, he had to forget completely about everything, switch off all unnecessary circuitry and concentrate only on what the computer wanted of him. And still he made mistakes. He didn't have this in his blood, like those youngsters, who grew up on technology.

It was growing dark outside, but the computer screen remained as bright as ever. Sometimes, Ludvík reached for a cigarette. From time to time he lifted the empty coffee cup to his lips, and then for a few minutes crushed the unpleasant grounds between his teeth — and then he even forgot about that. He was compiling a never-ending table in Excel, arranging eight-digit codes in their proper columns. He gathered them into his short term memory, and wrote in another place — *four six* — *three five* — *seven one* and *nine nine* — *four nine* — *eight three* — *eight two* and *seven eight* — *five one* — *three nine* — *seven eight*. By the third chain he knew for sure that he'd already forgotten the first one, and when he entered the next code: *three four* — *seven three* — *two five* — *one nine*, he forgot the second chain, and so it went for hours on end. The numbers swam through his head and he arranged them with absolute certainty. *Tomorrow, somebody's going to inspect this spreadsheet, and while they won't find a single error, I won't have in my head a single one of these numbers, which constantly, maybe every two seconds, exactly and impatiently I held there.*

Where are my numbers? Well, entered into the program… The last ones were, if I remember: five six — eight one — five nine — three four, but they've disappeared already. Where to? Ludvík asked himself, watching the columns of numbers as they disappeared through his head.

Where are my numbers? They have disappeared into the underworld of forgetfulness like unplayed notes. I am paid to shuffle thousands of numbers through my poor brain, numbers of which I know nothing. I'm like the musical scribes, who made copies of scores they never heard. No one wanted them to hear them. They might as well have been deaf. All that was required of them was clean penmanship, and thus in their ignorance they touched the summits of the musical art. They say that the entire Gospel can be found in the compositions of Johann Sebastian, and in their heads nothing more remained than there does in mine after the passage of these numbers.

Ludvík finished working. Carefully, he packed up his day's work, and powered down the computer. The darkening evening took possession of the room. He sat there for a little while, looking out the window at the falling snow and thinking about what he'd forgotten. And so he was thinking about nothing. He might just as equally have been thinking about what he'd remembered. Darkness was growing round about, *into which the bright flakes of our experiences and fear are borne away. Fear, which reaches the head as well as the heart. No theology will save you from that fear. You daren't think about it; you've got to turn your back to its abyss and move on.*

He got up from his chair. He turned on the ceiling light and checked to make sure that all of his machines were properly turned off. Then he entered the security code, and exited the place.

It would be even worse, he said to himself, as he walked through the impersonal corridors of the broad building, *if those numbers really existed, sorted and bristling like the teeth of combs in endless rows.* He walked through the gates and nodded to the female guard, who (obviously against regulations) had admitted the pedlar into the building in the first place.

He actually still wanted to go somewhere and buy something, but he wasn't feeling too well. He neither wanted to go to the shopping centre, nor home. *In that case...* before he knew it, he had entered the pub. It was called the Pelikán Bar. Maybe he just could sit here for a while in peace, as he used to do, when he still frequented pubs. He made his way to a table in the corner. Here, he was quite alone. There was only one fellow sitting at the bar, talking with a barmaid. It was the pedlar, who that afternoon had been hawking his orchestral scores to Ludvík. He'd covered the area, and now stopped in here for a vodka. Ludvík smelled the odour of cheap cigarettes, the kind that are smuggled in from Poland, circumventing the import taxes. *That's what he smelled of up there in the office; I said to myself that he stinks of that horrid weed, Karo, or whatever it's called.*

He ordered a white wine, just as he used to, when he frequented the pubs; a white wine, Müller Thurgau, and gazed again at the pedlar. At his blue paper box with the aluminium covered corners. He had it open on the bar, and was displaying its contents to the barmaid.

"You see, Ma'am, this here collection would be really nice. Songs from films and fairy stories. You don't have a CD player around here, by any chance?"

"No, probably not," the barmaid smiled. She was a woman of about thirty, with a beautiful oval face. A motherly sort of woman, sympathetic to her guests.

"Too bad. I wouldn't mind listening to them myself."

"What? You're not familiar with what you're selling?"

"In this case, actually, I have to admit that I'm not. My boss packed my case this morning without so much as a word. But these are films that all of us know: *Three Wishes for Cinderella, Saxána...*"[13]

---

13   *Three Wishes for Cinderella* (literally and unfortunately "Three Nuts for Cinderella,") *Tři oříšky pro Popelku* (*Drei Haselnüsse für Aschenbrödel*) a 1973 Czechoslovak/East German feature film directed by Václav Vorlíček; Saxána is the

All at once Ludvík noticed how fragile that man was. He had dirty hands: nails, knuckles, grubby cuffs. Those hands were not soiled with the good dirt that clings to strong, hard-labouring hands. No, his dirt ate away at the slender, lank hands like a sickness. Just like the deep shades of the wrinkles on his face. And those teeth hidden behind the thick droopy mustache — he'd rather not think of them. To all that, the obligatory rumpled suit and mangy tie, which slinked about his chest as if mocking its ornamental purpose. He had low-cut shoes on, splashed with mud. His hair and his beard were a little long.

Ludvík took a sip of his wine and looked at him through half-closed lids. *Who does he remind me of? Crap...* He thought about times past, when music was still sold on big black disks, in well-scuffed sleeves. *That's it. He looks like Paul McCartney on* Let it Be. *That's what Paul would look like today, if success and wealth had passed him by. If he hadn't broken through and had to hawk the unsaleable productions of Apple Records through the streets of Liverpool. Bitten, rusty apples, dry and wrinkly like the actual hero of the song "I'm a Loser."*

In a flash, the tones of that familiar song transported Ludvík back to his youthful years. A girl's face and a bit of anticipation and a savour on the lips... *and all of it's gone now. Six one — eight four — two five — nine three, or was it something else?*

"You know, Ma'am, it's tough with kids," the pedlar said to the barmaid who listened to him with empathetic attention. "...my second wife kept me from seeing him, as if he was no longer mine, which was proven true after all, and so I didn't have a chance at the divorce. And it didn't matter to her at all that I was the one who took him to handball and volleyball and to the movies and concerts... No access, and that's that!"

"That's real tough for you. Some people just don't get it," agreed the barmaid. She poured him another vodka and brought over another glass of wine to Ludvík. And she looked at him with such understanding as if to say *I don't really give a shit, but those boys are unhappy...*

"And yet that boy's already into hard drugs — that's what happens," said the pedlar, bringing the matter to a close.

---

heroine of a similar fairy tale film: *Dívka na koštěti* ("The Girl on the Broomstick"), Czechoslovakia, 1972, also directed by Vorlíček.

　　　　　　　　　　　　　　　　　　　　　

"That scares the heck out of me," shivered the barmaid. "I have a daughter, and I'm raising her alone but — knock on wood —" and here she rapped twice upon the bar, "she's an angel."

"I've got a daughter too," the pedlar rushed to put in his three cents in reply, and Ludvík himself wasn't far from piping up that he had a daughter as well, and an angelic one at that.

"My own daughter, from my first marriage," the pedlar went on. "She's got a future in front of her. But she has to choose if she wants to study psychology, or go into modelling. 'Cause she's a cutie, she is. She's probably on her own by now. I haven't seen her in quite a while. You know, what can I offer her, from this?" he said, thumping sadly with his hand on the box with the compact discs..

"Hand it over then, we'll put one on," the waitress suggested. "I think there might be a CD player in that stack over there. It's just that we've always got the radio going in here."

The radio went silent, and fairy-tale music filled the pub.

"How much do you get from one CD sold?" asked the barmaid, matter-of-factly.

"Twenty crowns. I sold ten today. So I'll make it to tomorrow, and treat myself to one more." He pushed the empty glass in her direction.

"I always tell myself that I shouldn't have left school. I was at the pedagogical institute. Could've been a teacher," he ended grimly.

"That wouldn't've made you rich either," the barmaid consoled him.

Twenty crowns. Two hundred for a whole day of tramping about with a box. Ludvík felt his knees tremble beneath the table. He looked at the pedlar and everything inside him turned around. *One CD — one shotglass. My God, what misery, at twenty crowns.*

"You know, Ma'am, I've just got to stumble onto the right guy. Someone who has money enough and interest and needs my music, for a store or a disco maybe. The sort of guy who'd buy maybe a hundred — the whole set, classics, country, orchestral scores. Then I'd be in like flint. More than once I've come across someone who bought even a hundred and fifty. Not today, mind. Or yesterday," he laughed.

Ludvík, who once had almost become a parson, couldn't forget what happened at the pool of Bethesda.

Sir, I have no man, when the angel troubles the water for healing, to put me into the pond. And here I have been laying for many years, called out the cripple to Jesus.[14]

Sir, I have no man. And what did Jesus say to that? Ludvík felt himself flush with heat, and his hands grow terribly weak. *What did he say? Arise and walk! Twenty forty — sixty eighty — one hundred one hundred twenty — one hundred forty one hundred sixty — how much you got on you?*

The pedlar pushed himself up from the bar. He grabbed his box and moved toward the door.

"Wait!" called the barmaid. "You've got one more disc here."

"Let it play. It's a gift from our company," the pedlar said with a wave of his hand before going out into the holiday darkness.

---

14   See John 5:1-15.

URŠULA

"Lounging in the tub again. I don't know what it's all about, but that woman of mine bathes probably three times a day," sighed Roman Hradílek expertly rotating the glass of beer they had just brought him. He just turned it on the porcelain tray and nodded calmly, as when someone playing *mariáš* calls out, *Colour? Good!*

"It's a bathing complex. Normal for women over thirty. Don't give it a second thought," his buddy Wagner reassured him. "My wife used to do the same thing before our divorce."

They clinked their glasses. The beer settled. The first one always settles like that. The afternoon began to turn to evening: five thirty, six thirty. *Three, four and then home. Just in time for the news.* They met here four times a week, between five and seven — a little social club of sorts. Only on Wednesdays they went to the local gym to play some football. A little something to keep you in form. And then to the pub until nine o'clock. Football makes you thirsty. Roman simply couldn't imagine the road home from work without a little detour to the pub.

"I don't blame you for that beer," his wife Uršula would say when she was blaming him for something else. "Yet it does bug me that you always want to avoid all the afternoon chaos."

With this she was thinking of children, tea, chores, shopping, the invasions of the mother-in-law, i.e. his mother, retired and bored, regularly dropping in on the young ones *who, for Pete's sake, aren't that young any more! No, you leave me to deal with all of that crap!* She was furious, and it pissed Roman off that Ula could so precisely formulate what he didn't want to express at all. That horrifying distaste of the flat in the afternoon. *Those idiotic hours, when I was supposed to be with them, I guess, and play the concerned Daddy.* So instead of that, he'd always say, "You're a woman, right? And so..." And the mother-in-law, the woman who bore him, would support him with a meaningful look of agreement, and then he and Uršula would scream at one another, locked in the bathroom, so that the children wouldn't hear them. The forced intimacy, the stifled hissing voices and the propinquity of Ula's body, red-hot with anger, always, despite the fury, aroused in Roman a desire to possess his wife amidst the quarrel. *In the nature of things* — said the burly sports physician to himself — *I ought to give Uršula a nice thrashing and then make love to her,* in this way combining rage and sex. But he never hit her. Only once had he gripped her forearm painfully, and then his unusually strong hands had left ugly bruises behind. Then he was afraid that she would wear short-sleeved shirts on purpose. But she wasn't like that. He made it up to her with a black turtleneck, which instead of revealing the bruises, emphasised her still fetching bust. Black turtleneck, jeans, hair pulled back in a ponytail, a handbag, and off to her friend for a Fernet. She looked just like she did in college.

When he was dating her in their student days, he was fascinated by the fact that he had no idea what was going on in that clever head of hers. She was a mystery to him, that girl, who spoke Czech, Polish and German fluently and had the whole Institute of Philosophy prostrate at her feet. He meanwhile was scarcely nibbling at his medical studies and was somewhat ashamed of the desire his working class parents had, to have a doctor for a son.

The witty golden youth of the student clubs back then liked to sing a little ditty, rather daring, for the times:

Up the shaft and down the shaft and what could there be finer?

Because my Papa was a doctor, I'm to be a miner!

Roman was so at sea with his position as a medical student, that he sang along with them. Even the second couplet, which ended with a phrase lifted from his own biography:

Because my Papa was a miner, I'm to be a doctor![15]

---

15   The tune was daring in that it poked fun at the class-based point system applied to the university application process in communist countries. Students from social classes traditionally under-represented in higher education, such as workers and peasants, received additional points in the application process. Because state education was free of charge, and the number of places available in a given year were often far less than the number of prospective students vying for admission, such points were often of great advantage to a person wishing to matriculate to a popular major field, such as law or medicine. At times, students from upper-class or intellectual backgrounds were denied admission

This was always greeted with a salvo of laughter. Uršula, who sometimes accompanied him to the club, would say, with her eyebrows arched above her chic round eyeglasses, that this foolery was little better than an exercise in Socialist self-incrimination. And he would shiver a bit with a thrill, and also with a little bit of anger, at how accurately she put her finger on it.

Later, her accuracy in detecting his self-incrimination became unbearable. At times she even seemed inhuman. As if with that brilliance or cool elegance of hers she was one important step in front of him. At last he freed himself from his constricted horizons and began to comprehend that things were otherwise than had been pounded into his head since he was small. But she had known that already for a long time, and it was as if she had no patience for his belated discoveries. Back then he sincerely hoped that together, they could somehow overcome it all. Uršula also hoped that Roman would somehow grow out of it. But each of them hoped on their own, and thus they remained, even when their children came along.

When she would return at night from a girlfriend's house, Roman was no longer surprised at anything. He understood her "leave me alone" and "don't touch me" perfectly. So they lay there next to each other beneath the eiderdown and felt fatigue slowly seeping into their lives.

It was eight thirty in the evening when she realised that she was lying in the bathtub for the third time that day, and that she felt like throwing up. Not from the adolescent clamour coming from her children, nor from the never-changing drone of her mother-in-law, who sat there in the kitchen, directing everything as she did almost every evening, until she grew tired of it, arose, and went back to the peace that remained her after the passing of her husband — *whom at any rate she ground to death beneath her heel.* No, she wasn't that bad after all. She even understood the woman, and was grateful to her in her way: at least she was somebody to talk to. And actually it didn't even bother her to see Roman parked in front of the TV again, at 7:30 exactly, well-oiled as usual. In the end that was better than him getting ideas. What

---

for that reason alone — and doctors' sons had little choice but to become manual labourers. See, for instance, the case of Václav Havel.

nauseated her was that she knew that the bath wouldn't help her, even before she poured it. *Neither hot nor cold, neither pink nor blue, to hell with it,* she said, and got in anyway.

That's the way it was with everything, at least from that day when she lost her job at the university and then, quite simply, just didn't look for another. *You know, work as a foreign correspondent in some private business firm — oh, what a prize that is! — translating idiotic e-mails for a couple of miserable crowns and worrying all the time about them kicking you out onto the pavement to make room for some young kitten. Thanks, but no thanks. Let the Good Doctor keep on making money, the Consultant, the Personal Trainer, even if he has some young kittens of his own to Personally Train — I don't blame him any more in the least.*

Hot water brought her nothing more than some sort of elemental sense of bliss. It also brought her drowsiness. *A woman who doesn't have a job tends to her family and goes to sleep. What else, since I have to account for every hundred crowns?* With mixed emotions she gazed at her daughter's cosmetics and — my God — those of her son, which gradually elbowed her own out of the space they occupied.

When they all left in the morning, Uršula didn't go to bed, nor did she get into the bath, as was her custom. She put on some nice clothes and did her face in the bathroom, not even paying attention to whether it was her cosmetics, or her daughter's, that she was using. In the foyer she bumped against Roman's dufflebags. The Good Doctor was going on a tourney with the rugby team. She laughed to herself. The time when she felt the temptation to rummage through her husband's stuff, looking for indications of this or that, passed long ago. These days she packed them herself. It was such a routine thing, that it didn't even occur to her. He only carried them near the door so as to have them on hand, when he should stop back here on the road from the centre.

You're not missing anything there? You'll be staying at a hotel. They'll take care of you there. "Up the hotel," you'll be staying, as you say it. Up the hotel, like all the illiterate yokels say… humph!

She went out into the street, and it seemed to her as if she were on her way to work. As if she was going to translate some books. *From Polish to German.* She'd like that the best. *The words would pass through this idiotic hole, from one place to another, like trains that never stop at such an unimportant station. I should never have got off here myself. It's all my own fault.* Then, suddenly, she felt bad for Roman and Romana and Robert and that mother-in-law of hers. *Poor souls. A slip of reason and life arises even there, where it has no reason to be. But that's the way life is. The sleep of reason produces not only moths, but little children and addle-brained old mothers and husbands, who would rather keep away in pubs or up the hotel.*

She went on thinking about herself, gaily, as if about someone else. She went to the store, even though there was nothing she needed to buy. Roman and his mother brought back a whole refrigerator full of food — but they had overlooked something, something was definitely missing from those duffle bags. She didn't know how to buy it. *Roman always bought it himself, even when they both needed it, and now he buys it and doesn't even pay attention to the fact.* She wandered among the aisles, unable to buy it just like that. She tossed things into the cart so as to slide it in among them, later, casually. *I'm a grown woman after all.* But no, she was like a stupid little girl. She took a bottle of wine, cheese, fruit. *As if for an intimate evening for two, with candles.* She picked up sanitary napkins and put them back again. *They don't go together with all that.* She ventured some laundry powder. *Disgraceful!* Just like toilet paper, bread, whatever. Suddenly, it all grew into an aesthetic problem. *What goes with it anyway?*

Nothing. She only bought that wine, fruit and cheese. She bought the condoms later at a gas station. *Fitting. At the pumps. Cigarettes and Durex, just like a whore.*

Back home, she opened up Roman's bag and slid the hard-won package into his toiletries bag along with the toothbrush and hand cream. *Now you're set*, she said, and left the flat again, determined not to return as long as those bags were still there.

CAROUSEL SWINGS

Swans? On such a dreary day? Sometimes it's dragons, which go better with the wisps of poisonous mist rolling among the prefabs. But those were swans bobbing up and down thanks to the hydraulics of the carousel swings. The air looks so thick, that even the silver piston rods pumping out of their hydraulic cylinders don't shine with their chromed steel finish, but remain matte grey, like extinguished fluorescent lights. But the thing is spinning after all. In the gloom of a late autumn day, a father sits with his child in the plastic shell of the swing between the swans' wings, high above the roof of the shopping centre, which was once called Rozlet.[16] *A big and a little person between heaven and earth; to believe in such a thing, you have to have the heart of a Hans Christian Andersen.*

Two women in long coats, with shopping bags in their hands, lift their gaze upward for a moment. Their eyes rest upon the laminated birds as if they were the most common thing in the world, just like the large and small merry-go-rounds, rollercoasters, caterpillars and swings, which stand there in the black and white gloom like some sort of forgotten enterprise. *Those two up there in the sky might provide the whole thing with some sort of sense, if they weren't so alone.*

"Is that a girl, or a boy?" asked Hans, lifting his eyes for a moment from the large mounted photograph.

"I don't really know," answered Bednář, the photographer. "I've given it some thought. It was so far away, and I didn't use a telephoto lens, on purpose. I wanted to capture the entire surroundings, and those two grandmas there in the foreground."

"I think it's a girl," Hans guessed.

"Actually, so do I. That the big one is a guy, you get that immediately, but the little one — like a little teddy bear."

---

16   There is a department store in Ostrava named Rozlet. Considering the general mood of these lines, there may be a subtle pun on the verb *rozlétat se*, which means "to go to pieces, fall apart."

"It's a beautiful picture," Hans concluded. He knelt on the floor again, among all the pieces being readied for Bednář's exhibit.

He much preferred to keep himself to these black and white photos, and strove to arouse in himself that — not fully comprehensible — emotion that he'd have to work into the catalogue text. In the same way, he had to take in the stifling atmosphere of the Bednář household. *If it must be*, he said to himself, and couldn't help but think that Alice Bednářová was sitting right now in the kitchen, drinking white wine and crying softly. The window looks out onto weather similar to that in the photograph, but without the swans, without the father and the little teddy-bear girl. *In a moment, she'll go off to the bathroom and there she'll repair, for a long, long time, the ravages of those tears. And Bednář the photographer will meanwhile smile a smile of seeming incomprehension, shrug his shoulders and perform all the antics performed by people who have a problem. So serious a problem that it cannot be spoken of, can only scream, slam doors, leave the house, get drunk. Do horrible things out of spite.*

Alice Bednářová, Alice Bednářová — those words won't be sticking together much longer, Hans said to himself, and gazed at the face of a man carrying some cracked plexiglass. Some poor soul in a cold arena. Cracks, welts and marks from pucks, hockey sticks and the helmets of hockey players are projected upon the face of an exhausted man earning a few crowns along with a gang of fellows similar to him, dismantling the rink in the multi-purpose sports hall, transforming it into tennis courts or a parquet floor for Latin dancing.

Everything is possible in this multi-purpose world. But those wrinkles round the eyes and mouth, those cracks, welts and marks, the pain of which sometimes strikes at the very heart, will only grow the deeper, the longer one lives.

Alice entered the room, bearing a tray with glasses and sandwiches. Boiled eggs, olives, paprika strips, ham — *and on top of it all she has to sweat over something like that, for God's sake.* She herself was fetchingly arrayed in a flowing brown house-dress which went well with her brown eyes. The traces of tears in those eyes could only be noticed by someone searching for them. Alice's feet — bare, save for the leather bracelet around one of her ankles — padded among the widespread photographs taken by her husband. Neither Bednář nor Hans moved. But Hans was moved, after all. *Who would not want a wife like that?* he said to himself.

Who, Bednář, wouldn't want to sit at the table, surrounded by one's work, since children are out of the question, and watch his beautiful wife carry up some food?

That would better fit a colour photo than a black and white. Only the bit about children I could have left out, Hans admonished himself for once more, once more, broaching in thought a matter which might look good, *Might — the absence of those cries at night, the absence of the threat of one's nest becoming a trap for a young pair of artists. To have children means the end of one's career. How stupid that sounds. Like from some idiotic soap opera retransmitted at three o'clock in the morning, when because of your insomnia you'll watch anything. Three years in the shithouse, and you'll fall out of everything. But not to have them, my God, and the whole world becomes an empty stomach, where there's room enough for everything, except a corner to snuggle in. One's bed is no longer a nest, but an airport, an international one at that, where each starts off from his own place in a different direction. Each unfaithful spouse with trembling knees thinks on that little piece of happiness… with someone else.*

Bednář, Alice, the things they say about you both! If even only half of it were true, you'd already have been done to death. And you, Alice, set a tray with splendid sandwiches on the table all the same and I stuff myself with them, as if I hadn't eaten for a fortnight, and I drink the wine over which you were just shedding tears in the kitchen. Carefully, I praise Bednář's pictures and meanwhile, mostly, I study your eyes to see that you're not pained by it. I look at Bednář and wonder if he senses it; and the only thing I sense myself is that you're both happy I'm here, because you won't quarrel until I leave.

Moments like these, which cry out for time to stop, are immeasurably dear to me. How you inconspicuously brushed my hand, and how your husband earnestly talks about his reportages, and how he is once more happily obsessed with his work as he was back then, when we walked about the old quarters of the town together with our cheap cameras and took pictures of broken windows and birches growing out of gutters. Well, he made it, and I found still other images, but those first focussings, those first exposures, we had together. In the end, that very first exposure, when the lens opens and the light falls upon the sensitive material of our souls, is common to us all, Alice.

Looking at Alice, Hans saw nothing but a woman. He looked at her beautiful, firm breasts, so clearly delineated beneath her loose dress;

at her full hips, her long legs. It seemed to him that the place shook, shivered, shakes again with the cry of a child, which only he can hear. It was so unbearable that he had to tear his eyes away toward Bednář's Karviná series.

Trampled traces on the pavement between the buildings, which were not left there, perhaps, by people. Some sort of machines beyond a fence. A bus shelter, in which some guy is waiting. He is so solidly grown into that frozen 1/60 of a second, that you hardly take notice of him. *Nor will you ever notice him as long as the scene remains static, as long as it is not shaken by a child's cry deep inside you; as long as you don't retrace those muddy footprints towards some safe place, to which you long ago bade farewell, lest you should freeze with that cigarette in your mouth and that briefcase in your hand, in that bus shelter, towards which at the moment no bus is making its way.*

They sat on for a little while longer and talked, about art rather than anything else. Alice was a promising singer, whose trained voice was just now searching for its proper timbre, or just settling, as one more accurately puts it, and that takes hours and hours of practice. She knows exactly what she's talking about. She has to sing, to appear before an audience, to work on herself. Bednář finds himself before his first major exhibition and doesn't know how it will all turn out. And Hans, their old friend, is supposed to work up some sort of text from it all. They ate the sandwiches, which either never diminished, or were unnoticeably replaced by Alice. Everything was OK up till then.

"You know, we're not quarrelling any more. We've already separated, really," Bednář told Hans as they walked toward the tram. And he pressed a great yellow envelope into his hands.

"This is for you. For that text," he said, and stood there on the little mid-road tram island, with hunched shoulders.

Hans knew what picture would be there, and it was. The photo with the swans. He just glanced inside the envelope; he didn't want to put on any show for the other people in the tram. When he looked into the paper cave with the picture of the carousel swings, all the emotions and confusion that he had experienced at his friends' apartment began to open up inside him. It was all caused by a memory that had slowly developed in his consciousness all that evening long.

He was nine or ten years old, definitely not older than ten. With a five-crown coin in his fist and his fist in his pocket, he shuffled towards the merry-go-rounds and the shooting gallery spread about the open spaces near his development. He was shivering with anxiety, because he was alone. He had no friends, neither then, nor ever. He could choose whatever he wished. He could hit the target at the shooting gallery and win a rose or a Disney figurine. He could take a ride on the carousel swings, where the children scream and grab one another's hands as they soar through the air. But his weak stomach wouldn't be able to bear that. He could go to the caterpillar or the Castle of Horrors, where at the end you get a whack on the head with a hairy tail. He'd prefer not to go anywhere, he was so frightened of these mechanisms and the people who crowded around them. But he had five crowns, and had resolved to come here by himself; the fact that his mother had given him five crowns brought tears to his eyes.

He bought himself a ticket for the children's carousel. It was a wooden turntable with little cars, motorcycles, horses, camels and giraffes. When he was small, he had never ridden on it. Now he was a little too big for it, but he was alone, and resolved. No one laughed at him when he sat himself down on a little green motorcycle. A little farther away a much smaller girl was sitting on a giraffe. Her daddy had set her down on it. He hunched down a bit, so as not to look so big. The bell rang, and the carousel began to turn.

Evening was drawing close. Lights came on in the distant houses. Most of the children held on to their rides solemnly — but none more seriously than little Hans. Here and there were the mysterious caravans of the carousel operators, which were known as temporaries, and thirsty little groups of bigger boys and girls, who perhaps were about to start something, together. All of this whirled about Hans, while he firmly gripped the handlebars, which had no control over the direction he was going in, and his heart began to hurt. Just as it did now.

AT THE COMMUNISTS

Leoš was sure that nothing could happen now, that all that bad stuff was behind him now, that it died along with his past life, and that now he was all right. *It's important to be all right, not to fear the next day, the next night. To calmly buy yourself a bottle of good Hungarian wine, sure, Egri Bikavér, and drink it, alone if you must, or with a female, whom you lead to the door tomorrow, with a smile, and close it behind her. All right. With a smile and a little something else, I don't have anything else for you, but what I gave you is quite enough. Three times a night, for sure. Four, no problem.* That's why he bought himself a nice wide bed. A real airport for long taxiing and sheer takeoffs. *It depends on what you're flying. I fly all sorts: from ultra-lights to B-52s. I've got something for them all. But mostly I prefer the F-16s, oh, those young rockets! — you can do whatever you like with them. They respond so well.*

There were times when Leoš felt like giving himself a pat on the back for his savvy in managing it all. He had climbed the rungs from teaching history at an elementary school to a university chair, and that's not all, by far.

On his way to work he stopped, as always, at the letterboxes in the hallway near the door. That morning, his trained eye caught on something white. He glanced through the round holes of the grey metal door of his letterbox, and saw a letter inside. Nothing strange about that: he got a lot of mail, letters, invitations to conferences, reminders from the library, but this one, it seemed, was different. The address was hand-written. *Yeah, by hand.* He stepped away from the letterbox. *Leave it. I'm not going to carry it around with me.*

A lot of time passed before he got around to that letter. Later on, when he was at last able to evaluate the events of that imminent day, he realised that the one thing he really wanted was to avoid that letter, ready and waiting in his letterbox. Perhaps it was the angle and shape of the handwritten characters. But something in the darkness of that tin letterbox must have terrified him.

After his final seminar he didn't want to go home at all. *Well then, I'll go through the park. There's no hurry.* At the far end of the park he stopped in at the pub named At the Cadaver. It got its name from the fact that the park had once been a municipal cemetery, and the pub stood on the place of the old mortuary. *I'll just have a seat, drink a beer, read the news, maybe somebody'll be there.*

But the sign on the door read "Closed — Renovation."[17] He look in through the glass and saw some hard-working Vietnamese turning the old Cadaver into an Asian bistro.

So, where to now? Hesitating, he looked around the bleak, uncongenial park. *What's closest to here?* Closest was a pub he'd never been in before. A proper person never goes in there, not even a proper drunk. It was called the Pub at the Cherry Trees. It was also called At the Communists, because the Party actually owned the building. Its very existence seemed so absurd to Leoš, that it never really entered his conscious mind. *There's a lot of such stuff around here*, he said to himself, shivering suddenly, all numb with cold and the disquiet arising in him from the suppressed thought of the letter in the letterbox. *Things don't stop existing just because they seem to be impossible.*

The pub was in a villa on the edge of the park. Upstairs were the offices of the Party rag, and down below the taproom and a hall. *Just like the good old days, before victorious February.* At the tables sat a few grandads and grandmas, who probably still remember that old carp Klému, who knew how to handle class enemies,[18] and a group of young people, who looked proper enough at first glance. And yet meeting their glance he felt an icy shiver course up and down his spine. It wasn't a very good idea to come here. He looked at the men and women sitting beneath the picture, or rather the reproduction of a frame from Eisenstein's *Battleship Potemkin*, and was aghast at the sudden urge he felt to go over to them, talk with them, sit among them.

---

17   There is a little ethnic jab in the original Czech, which reads *Zavženo — lekonstrukce.* The first word is misspelled (it should be *zavřeno*), and the second word, obviously, is *rekonstrukce,* the misspelling of which plays on the stereotypical idea that speakers of Asian languages have a hard time distinguishing "r" from "l."

18   Klement Gottwald (1896—1953) Head of the Czechoslovak Communist Party, first head of the Communist postwar state of Czechoslovakia, after the seizure of power in 1948. Like most Communists of the Stalinist years, he is remembered for a harsh, repressive rule.

                                        JAN BALABÁN

Idiots with complexes, he calmed himself, but then again something seized him, as it had done at the letterbox. *The word "idiot" written in Cyrillic. In Russian, it means* inmate. *A colony of unfriendly people named Gorkovo. Those were the times when the buckle on the belt of the teacher Semyon Makarenko[19] glittered in the sun of the new age and the villains were put under the gun. Education by the collective. They can get sentimental about such bullshit, who've never experienced it on their own skin! They have those old bosses so deep inside them, in their marrow, in their genes that, without even knowing why, they creep here to such meeting places decorated with the portraits of evil old men and paranoid leaders?*

And then he knew exactly what was hidden behind that word "boss" — the most vulgar of all Russian words, *mat'* — *Yeb tvoyu mat'* [20] *rodinu.*

He sat down at a corner table and looked at those black and white, or rather brown and white, photos on the walls and felt nauseous. He cheered himself with ironic chains of thought concerning how this pub is really proof of contemporary democracy, if only in virtue of the fact that in any Communist régime, all of those pictured on the walls would never be seen together. *They'd have knocked one another off. The only one missing here was Trotsky. The only true revolutionary. Trotsky, with his idea of permanent revolution, who plays in Communist mythology the role of the zealous heretic, like Jan Hus in the Church, or Joan of Arc. She too was only concerned with God's will; they couldn't not have burnt her at the stake.*

The portrait of Ché Guevara passed before him on the t-shirt of a lanky, unkempt kid. *He's dead in Bolivia, yet his soul is marching on.* He couldn't laugh at it, even if he wanted to. Even back then in the days of the so-called Revolution he couldn't laugh when his friends in their red neckerchiefs staged all sorts of recessive funerals of Communism. Leoš always thought such things should be talked about seriously, rather than running about in Pioneer skirts showing off one's hairy legs.

---

19   Anton Semyonovitch Makarenko (1888—1939). Controversial Soviet paedagog, who developed the use of self-governing childrens' collectives to exert "positive peer pressure" on the individual. Gorkovo was one of his institutions.

20   The word in question signifies "mother," the phrase in Russian is a common, and rather salty, curse which includes the word.

Sunk in these murky thoughts, he didn't even notice how he had progressed to hard drinking. With each beer, he had a double vodka. He fell inside himself and felt how all the seals and twine that he had so diligently trussed himself up with over five years were coming undone.

Five years ago, he had really thought that it was all over for good. Back then at the crematorium, when with so much effort he pushed those tears out of his eyes. You're supposed to cry when your mother dies, so he did. He laboured at those tears. And then he really did start to weep, overcome with himself, because over her casket, over her metal urn, at last he dared admit to his mind that this should not have been permitted him. That he simply shouldn't be so left without her, to do as he pleased. He read that in her grim eyes back then, at her hospital bed; he felt it in the abrupt movement of her hand, suddenly become so weak. That slowly dying, but smouldering expression of blame, which lasted to the very last moment, and which was taken from her face only by the flames of the furnace. *A furnace for people. Mummy.* He tossed the vodka down and ascertained with fright that the image of Joan of Arc was stuck before his eyes — that brutally shaven woman with the noble heart, the woman bound to the stake. The woman who does not forgive, because she knows that she will not be forgiven. That's how she looked at his father, when he did not recover from his stroke. That's how she looked at the television, when the Husák régime fell.[21] An abandoned old Communist, among opportunistic vermin. And the most treacherous vermin of them all — her son.

What do you people know about Communists? You've never lived among them. All you did was bow down before them, crawl up their arses while behind their backs you laughed at them like those lächelnde Bestien of Heydrich.[22] Your Mummy never took you by the hand to a

---

21   Gustáv Husák (1913—1991). Slovak Communist, head of the Communist Czechoslovak Republic from 1969 (when he reimposed a hard-line Communist régime after the brief "Prague Spring" of Alexander Dubček, brought to an end by the Soviet-led invasion of Czechoslovakia), until the late 1980s and the "Velvet Revolution" that brought four decades of Communist rule in Czechoslovakia to an end. He converted to Catholicism on his deathbed.

22   Reinhard Heydrich (1904—1942). Nazi official, one of the architects of the Holocaust. He was "Reich Protector" of Bohemia and Moravia from September 1941 until he was executed by Czech and Slovak soldiers in May of 1942. It was he called the Czechs "laughing beasts." He was quoted as saying "The Poles are hard

political meeting or to a First of May parade out of conviction. You didn't have to listen to the International played on the turntable at home in ten foreign languages, even fucking Mongolian! You didn't have to sign up to the Soviet Pioneers and look forward to Happy Pictures,[23] fuck it all!

"Yeah, one more double, please."

I c'n toss off at home under the covers on the airport even drunk. Three, four times a night, no problem. Of course, Leoš can do it, Leošek. Leoš, after Brezhnev, of course, Leonid Not fucking Emperor Leopold, first or second![24] I don't have the good heart of an emperor. Don't have a good one, or a bad one. Don't have any at all.

The left-leaning crew of the dingy pub looked on with amusement as that unknown fellow kept mumbling something or other over his vodka.

He had no idea how he got home. The damned letter, obviously, was still in the letterbox. Miracles don't happen. It shone there like some sort of radioactive substance to which it was wise to give wide berth; but no arc was wide enough to pass this one by. He opened the letterbox and pulled it out. With half-closed, drunken eyes he unwillingly scanned the lettering on the envelope. No, no, impossible. Have to end it all.

He went out in front of the building, opened the ashcan and, turning his face nicely aside, tore the letter into pieces. Then he slammed down the lid. I hope they cart it off tomorrow before I get up. But it was not meant to be; this night was not the end of it. The envelope had no sooner been torn than Leoš knew that all his tearing only intensified the pain of the message emerging from it. He sensed that the fragile wall he had been building so diligently since his mother's death was starting to crumble. His freedom, his historical perspective, his co-eds and his pretty doctoral candidates, his travels abroad to Holland and Scotland, all of these were mere toys, a childish barrier, flowers without roots stuck in the sand and protected by a little fence of sticks. Built by

---

and unyielding, and as such are easily crushed by force. The Czechs are spineless. They bend under pressure like a reed, but snap stiff again when you least expect it."

23   Весёлые картинки, a Russian Communist children's magazine, published monthly since 1956.

24   The references are to the Habsburg Emperors Leopold I (1640—1705) and Leopold II (1747—1792), not the Belgian monarch.

little Leošek on the little path, on the road that will soon be trampled by cattle, real cattle. Not little cow figurines delicately pushed about by a child's hand, but real cows, whom uniform breeding has transformed into one cow of a thousand heads, and the hooves of that animal, driven between electrified fences of historical necessity will trample flat an innumerable number of fences placed along the path by naive little boys like me.

Leoš pawed about the room after that bottle of wine. *But wine won't drown it. You'd need a sea of wine for that, more than a sea, a Baikal Lake of vodka; you'd need to get pissed like they do in Russia, like the hopeless Yakuts and Samoyeds, with no shamans and no spells, drunk among their empty tins of conserves. Notorious drunks in the tin hovels allotted them by revolutionary might. That's might for you.*

Leoš gabbed his elbows and closed up tightly within himself, in an effort to somehow squelch the furious rhetoric in his head. He couldn't defend himself any more; the next step would perhaps be towards the window.

He lay down on his bed. No sooner had he closed his eyes than he heard her stifled breathing. It was a sound not fully human. She did that to him, often, when he was a child. Even when he was a child, just discovering the possibilities of his body in the bathtub, she always did that to him. All three of them slept in the narrow bedroom. Leoš's bed was pushed close to the foot of his parents' conjugal bed. He didn't know why he couldn't sleep in the living room or in the kitchen. But he didn't dare suggest it. She'd never allow that. She wanted it that way, and she always had it the way she wanted. She was a Communist, and she knew what was good for people. And so she never hesitated at night to pull her husband, Leoš's father, close to her large bosom, enclose him between her thighs and shake him against herself. That breathing, that groaning! When Leoš once peeked over the headboard of their bed, he just saw a huge eiderdown, which trembled like a mountain. Magnitude seven on the Richter scale. His father had to be in there, somewhere; his father who, before the trembling began, always whispered "No, no, the boy is here." But his mother was inexorable. He read that in his father's eyes. Inexorable. His father began to wear away and it was she who regulated that, his withering and his paling and his fragility. How similar they were, he and Leoš.

One night (Leoš was already fourteen and knew well what his parents were doing; a pal of his showed him photos from a German magazine; Leoš's head was aswim with those images, and rage — full of determination to spit on everybody and do something bad), when all that jerking and groaning was getting underway he got out of bed and walked over towards the door. He wanted to get away from all that. In the bathroom, because that door could be locked. Out of the house entirely, if only he had a key. He had taken just two steps before he heard his mother's voice. Not a whisper, but a full, imperative command: "Where are you going!"

He stood there stiff as a nail struck on its head and driven into the wood.

"To the kitchen," he assayed a reply.

"No you're not. Get in bed, now!" she yelled.

And his father? Not a peep out of him. But he was there. A Yakut, a Samoyed, helpless in the arms of the she-bear. (Even so Leoš understood how important it was that his father was there, somewhere, anywhere, weak and fragile, but *there* all the same). Obediently, he crawled back into bed and waited until the trembling mountain was stilled. He lay there in the deep shadows and despairingly tried to think of nothing, to be nothing. And it worked. That night he learned that he not only knew how to shut his eyes, but also to shut down his brain. And he shut it down every night after that.

And tonight, tonight, it all opened up again. He lay there loosely on the airport runway, which replaced the old conjugal bed of his parents, breathing heavily as if after sex, and quite calmly thought it was all over. He had believed that he was finally mature, and completely forgot about the letter, the fragments of which the dustmen were at that very moment shaking into the depths of their truck along with the other rubbish.

The next few days flowed by in perfect peace. Leoš twisted off a brutal hangover following his private little flameout At the Communists, and didn't have too much of a desire to touch anyone, or anything. He let his co-eds and his pretty doctoral candidates alone. He even cancelled his tutorials on silly pretexts, just so that nothing would disturb him and his newly-obtained consciousness. He wandered about the streets, drank tea or coffee in the pubs he visited, and suddenly began to take notice of each corner of the familiar city as if it were something completely new. At last he began to think about what was going on with him. He didn't want to pose any diagnoses, although quite a few presented themselves to him. He felt that something was on its way to him, and he didn't want to scare it off.

On Friday evening he went nowhere. He merely leafed through an unorthodox study which posited that the rise of Stalinism in Russia actually helped on the acceptance of Nazism in Germany. *There's something to that. So scared of Bolshevism were they, that the people chased out an imp only to replace him with Satan himself. The whole twentieth century might be explained in this way.*

Then the doorbell rang. That didn't happen often. He wasn't used to unannounced visits. *Maybe it's a neighbour.* He opened the door just as he was, in sweats and an old striped t-shirt. A woman was standing there. A woman such as he'd never laid eyes on before. Small, at first glance energetic, on the right side of forty. *Full, so to speak.* Black hair, maybe a tad dyed, French cut, at the level of her jaw. She was dressed in a modern fashion, but matter-of-factly, the way managers or doctors dress. Her eyes were dark, deep, a little wild.

"I'm Elena," she said instead of a greeting. "My last name won't tell you anything. That's why I didn't even write it down."

The letter. That rejected, unopened, shredded letter was suddenly back again. Those twisted handwritten characters, so similar to his own. It even crossed his mind that maybe he'd gone nuts, and had sent the letter to himself. And those eyes of hers. He had the same kind of eyes. It was like looking into a mirror.

She seemed amused at his fright. She stepped into the foyer of his flat uninvited.

"You didn't get my letter?"

"No, I just…"

"Well then, you must be surprised indeed." She looked at him as if he were a little boy.

"So then, first thing is to explain it all to you," she continued, matter-of-factly again. "I'm Elena, your older sister. We have the same mother."

"There must be a mistake," he stuttered, stupidly, although her very looks excluded the possibility. Only that elegance of hers, and the openness with which she offered him her hand, were not his mother's. But her handshake was firm, like hers.

"I didn't know that I had a sister. To tell the truth, I'm sort of knocked off balance. Pardon me," he said, letting go of her hand, which he had held in his own for an unnaturally long time.

"Nobody knew about it," she explained knowingly. Suddenly, her voice was harder. "She kept me hidden from everybody. I was raised by my father and grandmother."

"I didn't even know that my mother was married before."

"She wasn't."

"And so, how did it come about?" he said, like a complete idiot.

"Well, you know. Sometimes people aren't who they seem to be, Leo. We gonna stay here by the door?"

"No, no, come in. Here, in the kitchen. The living room's a mess. Here, sit down, please."

"You live alone?" she asked, taking a seat at the kitchen table.

"Yeah, alone."

"Me too. Again. Will you make us some coffee?"

"Sure! Coffee… coffee…"

Feverishly, he prepared two coffees, as if that spinning spoon could somehow calm down the maelstrom in which he found himself. That sudden thrill. Unimaginable. His mother's porcelain was rattling in his hands.

"I know this must be a shock for you," she said, comprehendingly.

She's a doctor for sure. A doctor or a manager. Doctor, manager, doctor he repeated in his head.

"I didn't really know our mother. But when my father died, and I had no one else in the world, I began to look around for her — and I found you."

She smiled at him and it occurred to him that he must certainly know her, his sister, *his sis.*

"So," he said, setting the coffee on the table before at last succeeding in getting a proper sentence together, "So mother in effect abandoned you… ma'am."

"Yeah, I'm an abandoned child," she laughed. "And stop with the formalities, OK?[25] We're siblings after all. She left me with my dad and disappeared. At first, I thought she was dead. Dad never told me

---

25   *Nevykej mi.* Since her appearance at his door, Leoš's sister had been using the informal second-person singular address (*ty*) used with friends and family

anything about her. But when I was bigger he told me that she had left us, that it had been a mistake. He didn't say nice things about her. I had the feeling that he was afraid of her. Forgive me — your experience must be different. When I was small I called my grandmother Mama."

"Well, experience, experience…. She died more than five years ago. I had just been thinking about that, and here you are! Shall we have some wine?"

Leoš brought in the Bear's Blood from the living room.[26]

"Bear's blood. Nice brand. Good sign," Elena laughed as they clinked glasses. "To mother?"

"To us, rather," Leoš suggested shyly.

And so they talked for a few hours, in a way that no two other people in the world could talk. Their experiences mixed in together. Everything was backwards, and everything was right. The whole bottle of Leoš's red wine was emptied.

Elena, Elena — Leoš felt so surprised by the realities lying past the boundaries of life. Past those electrified fences of historical necessity a whole, free country spreads wide. Elena, the doctor with his mother's eyes and sharp gestures — fortunately! — knows nothing of her. In the hospital, dressed in green scrubs, with her precise instruments, she realises her mother's immense potential for good, of which that old woman hadn't the slightest idea.

He knew that he was babbling a little, but he wanted to babble. He wanted to laugh and babble to his heart's content. He was laughing with his sister, in a way that Leoš had never laughed before, laughing right in the face of life, in its very eyes.

"I can't stick with anybody very long," she said. "Something starts to bug me, and before you know it, it's over."

"And I've never found anybody that I'd like to live with."

"Have you ever looked for one?"

Her gaze sank into him deeply, dangerously. But there can be no danger where there is nothing to protect.

"No. I've really never wanted anyone like that."

---

members. He on the other hand had reflexively referred to her in the polite, second-person plural (*vy*).

26   Bear's Blood is a Bulgarian red wine. Earlier in the story, Balabán had spoken of the Hungarian red wine Egri Bikavér, which is translated Bull's Blood.

Elena didn't want to sleep over. She had a room in a hotel and all that.

"We shouldn't overdo it with this brother- and sisterhood," she laughed. "We're complete strangers, after all."

He walked her to the hotel and, suddenly, embraced her at farewell. He sensed that he had a woman in his arms — the only woman in the whole world. He sensed her meeting him halfway. In that moment, he wanted to suggest that everything was possible. After all, nobody knows that they're brother and sister. They could, they could… do anything.

It lasted for a few seconds. And then she carefully, but firmly, unwound herself from his embrace.

"Don't worry," she said at goodbye, "we won't lose each other again."

HIS MASTER'S VOICE

"I do believe that that dog has something of the terrier in him. Really, at least a few drops of sly hunter's blood, those crafty abilities to lead an armed man on a horse toward animals bigger and stronger than himself. And hold him, hold him at bay, deafen him with barking, perplex him with feint and subterfuge, phoney attacks, phoney courage. Snapping and leaping and all the while counting the moments until the horse broaches the thickets, and his master raises his gun and the beast falls at the feet of the little dog.

"To conquer, you need the help of a man. And for that reason, you've ceased to be an animal yourself. The instincts imprinted in your blood summon forth the picture of a man, who follows in your tracks. A man in a green coat — a hunter's jacket, the covering of a forest warden, who doesn't hesitate to send you after a bear, even — or a red coat — the overcoat of a nobleman, who chases the fox along with you, just for fun. Or maybe even a lady in an elegant hunter costume, or a poacher in mottled hood. He — or she — is always behind you, hearing your bark and appearing just in time to kill instead of you. And if it happens that he's delayed, you'll die torn apart by the wild animal, but still firmly believing that he will still arrive after all, even if after you're dead.

"Thus proclaims your genetic code. And it also says that your food will not be the hot blood and flesh torn from the belly of the given prey. It's tripe you'll eat, offscourings that your master tosses to you, after he's consumed the good bits. The hunt is over — here's your wages. Off-slicings, tinned dog food, biscuits, kibble in a tin bowl. You need a human hand to dispense your food.

"You carry man about inside you, and yet you will never become a man. You frightful hybrid, you. You risk your life for someone who values his own life above the lives of all dogs taken together. Who drowns without a wink your feeble, malformed puppies, who pours out to the dogs what he himself finds contemptible, and who, in his imaginings, incomprehensible to you, has more respect for the wolf you abandoned when, on the path of your development, you went off after your god. And lo your god, the poet of the *Jungle Book*, apostrophises the death of his hero with the words "Howl, dogs! A Wolf has died tonight!" And so you howl obediently, and when you do, all the village wiseacres will laugh and say that you're calling to your friend on the moon.

"I feel for you, you hopelessly pious creature, whenever I see you on the circular sticker of the black record, attentively listening to the recorded voice emerging from the metal trumpet of the old-fashioned phonograph, intent on recognising your master's voice amidst the hisses and pops."

Hans was sitting on the shoe locker in the foyer, blabbing like an evangelical pastor, gazing into the little dog's eyes, among whose forebears there surely had been some fox terriers. This garrulousness, which is characteristic not only of more than one pastor, but of almost all those confessing to that god-fearing denomination, notably got on the nerves of Anna Marie (Catholic, at least as far as her baptismal certificate is concerned). In that otherwise broad heart of hers, as broad as it was deep, there was yet no place for the cascades of words with which the Protestants vainly strive to lay their anxiety and guilty conscience, for not daring, on dogmatic grounds, to recognise any authority save that of the Highest. And yet they close themselves off from any chance at approaching Him through this inability of theirs to shut up at least for a moment, so as to give ear to His soft voice.

All the same, this gabbiness agrees somehow with the intensity of their spiritual lives. It's an excessive growth, which they drag behind themselves like a hunchback — just like Catholics do their superstition and attachment to any authority, over which one can scribble a halo.

Beyond confessional distinctions, though, what really bugged her was the way her husband, in his hangover, exalted himself above the dog, as if it were a mere worm. Who else would seek to assert his dignity above that of an unfortunate, stray animal, and in such a refined way, as if he expected a confession of solidarity and understanding?

But two things don't jibe here, or really three, it occurred to Anna Marie in a self-critical reflection. First, Hans wasn't hung over. Or else that hangover had been going on for almost a year — from that very day when he stopped drinking. He's having, rather, one of his regressive flashes, when something like drunkenness comes upon him, without his having ingested even a drop of booze. As he says himself: the brain has learned it by rote, and sometimes it just carries on like that through muscle memory.

Second, he's sitting there in the foyer, on the boot locker, behind the closed door — where he always sat — and he'd be surprised to think that anyone besides the dog was hearing what he was saying. Nor was it true that — what originally angered Anna Marie — that via his sermon to the dog he was speaking — he, the master of parables — to *her*, spitting back her own words of devotion and the ties of blood. For they had no children together. Each of them had a child with someone else, from the first marriage, as one says, and all these words of genetics and ties of blood were hurtful to her.

And third, Hans certainly didn't imagine that the dog understood him, and so he was actually talking to himself. In his metaphors and parables he's vainly searching for a narrow passage between his Scylla — the faithful dog — and Charybdis — the wild wolf — only to discover with horror, that no such passage exists. *You can be this, Hans, or that. You can envy the dog his master, or the wolf his freedom. Oh, how well do I know that!* Anna Marie whispered to herself standing there with her ear close to the foyer door, while being at the same time as far from there as the moon is above the mountains.

Her fingers were already near the handle, so as to bring this moment with Hans/without Hans to a conclusion, when she backed away from the door on tiptoe. She wasn't a fan of sudden sentimental embraces, and everything seemed to be heading that way at the moment.

Their dog Tom, who was at the moment sitting at Hans' feet like a diligent pupil and literally paying attention to each word that came out of the mouth of his master, was a foundling. According to the veterinarian's best guess, he was at least seven years old, which in the case of a dog means that he'd lived through the better half of his life, with someone else. They had no idea who that person was. So, during those first seven years, he had supposedly loved someone else. Maybe he had suffered. Rather, for sure he wasn't treated kindly. Judging from how nervous he was, skittish and touchy, his life couldn't have been a simple one.

At the start, he fawned over Hans. Perhaps he sensed in him a sort of authority. But then very quickly, he chose Anna Marie as his favourite. He loved her so much that soon he began to practically warn away from her all of the other members of the household. When she returned home from work, he threw himself upon her, jumping up very high, leaping up her dress, tugging at her stockings, and there was no way to calm him down. When he was to go on his evening walk with someone other than her, with Hans for example, he always made sure that everyone was aware of his contempt and disgust. Even though he walked the first metres as if involuntarily, his legs were unbent, as stiff as sticks. This reminded Hans of a child's toy — a little wooden drummer fixed to a tiny cart, pulled by a string. His arms were fixed to the bent axle of the rear wheels, and the faster one pulled the cart, the faster would he batter the little tin drum before him. So it seemed to Hans that he was pulling along just such a toy, and it made him feel like a tastelessly overgrown and cruel baby.

And from this it was just a tiny step to a memory of a difficult moment, which he and Anna Marie had experienced at the start of their relationship. At first, Anna's five-year-old daughter couldn't bear his visits. She fought tooth and nail with him over her mother, whom she wished to have for herself alone. *Mama, make him go away!* He wasn't fond of remembering that. Once, when they were sitting in the kitchen discussing their future — much of which couldn't be seen, at the time — Anna's daughter brought her toy piano into the room and set it on the table between them. Then she began to pound it, just as resolutely and mechanically as that toy drummer, just so they wouldn't be able to talk. *Oh, life is hard when the blood boils like a flooding stream…*

Tom didn't remain in his own stream bed either. The dog was afraid of thunder and any sort of loud boom. Whenever he heard a blast, he tore off without a second thought. Once, he ran away in a thunderstorm, leaving behind him all of his unknown past. He turned up soaked to the skin and dejected on the outskirts of the city at the doors of a "gentlemen's club" called Club Chloé. He never had it as good as he did there, stroked by so many beautiful goddesses. He lay down before them on his back, rode the bike with his hind leg… He could have become the darling of the whole place. Yet here he had two rivals, great big English Mastiffs, who guarded the shady locale and whose one constant desire was to tear little Tom in pieces.

And this is how it came about that the owner of the girly club asked his friend the money changer to find a home for the cute little dog, and the money changer mentioned the dog to a real estate agent of his acquaintance, and he passed the news on to his wife, a passionate dog lover — and she, at last, to Anna Marie, who had been longing for a dog for a while now.

One afternoon — the owners insisted upon it being in the afternoon — Anna and Hans visited the bordello Chloé, and when the Madame, dripping with gold, was convinced of the fact that they were good people and that they'd take good care of the little dog, they were allowed to take him away. Moreover, they also got a leash and a vaccination certificate, which that good soul had taken care of herself. As they were going away, a tear of real emotion sparkled in her makeup-plastered eye.

They called the dog Tom after the well-known foundling Tom Jones from the novel by Henry Fielding, as he had also found a haven among ladies of easy manners during a difficult period.

"I think that he's finally happy at our house," Anna Marie said, when she had liberated Hans from the foyer, where he was experiencing his phantom hangover.

"If so, it's just because he can't remember his earlier life," Hans said in reply.

"And why should he? He's a dog. He doesn't have to remember."

"You're right. He doesn't."

"Why should he torment his mind with the past and the future? He's happy *now*, and he's grateful for it, and that's what I like about him."

"He doesn't even know who he belongs to."

"What do you mean he doesn't? I think he knows quite well. Just look how calmly he's lying there. He's safe; he doesn't want to be anywhere else; he's got everything he needs."

"Maybe. And maybe it's all just an act. Maybe all day long he's in despair, tensing his ears in anticipation of finally hearing his real master's voice," Hans said.

"Not everybody has to be as vain as you are," Anna Marie said in response.

Hans knew she was right, but he couldn't do anything about it. So he got up and took that lost dog out for some exercise, at least.

PYRRHULA PYRRHULA

The climb to the top of the ridge cost him all his breath. The slope, overgrown in yellowed grass, was so steep, that when he bent down, he could touch the path before him. Each step lifted him up, appreciably, as if he were on a staircase, or a ladder. When he glanced down into the valley, he saw that the cabin, which they had left just about an hour before, was distant and small — as can happen only in high mountains. The wind chased away the clouds, and the side of the mountain, overgrown in sparse, wind-buffeted beeches, was drenched in sunlight. Michal took a deep breath before the next step. He looked up above himself, where in the rays of the sudden sun glittered the tensed calf of his wife Věra. *That's how she is. A competitive animal, a mare who can't walk alongside someone, because she's always got to be at least a little in front.*

They neared the very top of the ridge. Věra looked back. It seemed to Michal as if a smile had flashed across her face. She pointed upwards, but the words she said were torn away by the wind. Michal asked himself what they would do, if that summit were still a few unimaginable thousands of metres higher. *Each of us would probably drop where we were, leaving our bodies to lie here forever, at exactly this altitude, at which we've arrived just now.*

After a moment, both of them met at the summit of the sharp ridge, which divided one abyss from the other. The brisk wind clung to their sweating skin. They seemed to be naked; like some kind of creatures other than people, when they embraced, resting chest upon chest, and breathing heavily past the other's shoulder. Michal felt Věra's heart beating, as if he didn't have one of his own.

Then they retreated to a little sheltered depression overgrown with dwarf pine and alders. They drank some water and ate their bread and cheese. Michal stretched out on his back and gazed up at the sky which, from the east was burdening over with dark clouds, which disturbed the heretofore sunny weather. *Just a bit, and we'll be chattering our teeth in mist and downpour. Just a bit, and we'll be screaming words of reproach at one another, our eyes bulging in fury.*

He watched Věra change into a dry t-shirt. He watched her braid her spreading hair, and wipe her sweat-covered glasses with a paper tissue.

"Look at those birds — how red they are," Věra said, pointing with her hand toward a dwarf alder, on which some small birds had alighted. Red-bellied, they chirped through strong beaks. "Are they robins?"

"Bullfinches," replied Michal, who, in his childhood, had belonged to a birdwatcher's group. *Míša.* Back then he was certain that he'd become a veterinarian one day, and an illustrator of nature atlases. In his notebook, he drew pictures of every bird he came across.

"When I was a little girl, they would alight on our balcony. After Christmas, we would spread crumbs and stale cookies on the ledge for the birds. Mama always baked more than we needed. Birds like that would fly up for them — I always thought they were robins. I don't think I've seen one since I was a child."

"Maybe you just haven't looked for them. They fly up on our ledge all the time."

She looked at him, as if only now she had noticed his presence. Her eyes fixed on Michal with the same involuntary absorption as the eyes of a little girl fixed on red birds against the grey-white background of a city courtyard, past the window.

The wind gusted, and the bullfinches flew off. Without the counterpoint of their red feathers, the green of the alder leaves suddenly became dull.

Before them rose the mountain called Stoh.[27] Bald and full. Golden meadows and rubble. Bands of purple-blooming verbein pushed upwards toward the summit of the gigantic cone. More than a haystack, it resembled the summit of a great heart, turned upside down.

Mist was rising up from the valley to the right. It didn't flop over the ridge onto the valley on the left, but rose straight up, as if obeying an invisible partition that divided the space. The valley on the right was full

---

27 Stoh, a mountain of 1,324 metres in the Krkonoše range in the North Central region of the Czech Republic, near the border with Poland. Known as *Heuschober* in German, the name of the mountain, *Stoh*, means "hayrick."

of mist, while that on the left was clean and deep, with those touching little houses and cottages and flocks of sheep at the foothills. And at the borderline of the clearly seen world and that other, suspected one, where the clouds met with the bright current of sunrays, two figures in windbreakers were moving along, one behind the other, yet holding hands, as if one were leading the other.

"When I was twelve years old, in sixth grade, I found a dead bullfinch. It was lying beneath the wall of our building, draped in its wings, as if it were asleep. I picked him up. He was soft in my hand, and beautiful. He must have died just a moment before I came across him, because he wasn't stiff at all. He was soft, round, I would say. He filled my whole palm. I felt bad for him, and at the same time I had the feeling that he wasn't really dead; he was so intact; he was somehow all mine. You know what that's like. You like a person or a thing chiefly because of the fact that you yourself found it, or him, yourself. And that's how that dead bullfinch came alive in my hand. I couldn't part with him. I took him home, and kept him hidden in a coat pocket until my mother found him."

"What did she say?"

"She said it was dangerous. That there might by any number of infections that you could get from him, and that we should have a funeral for him. And I acted like a nut. I put him in an old shoebox and tried to come up with a way of keeping him. At last I lit upon the thought of having him stuffed. There were a lot of stuffed birds in a cabinet at school. A whole tableau made up of stuffed titmice, swallows, swifts, finches and shrikes, against a painted background of woods and sky. I wanted something like that for myself."

"You still do, don't you?" Věra interrupted him, a flash of sunlight reflecting to him from her glasses as she looked back at him over her shoulder.

"Well, that's not completely true," Michal pulled back, recalling in his mind those pictures of his, which he transferred from his childhood notebook to sizeable canvasses, beneath the weight of which he almost collapsed, at that moment.

"Back then I knew more precisely, and that's why I asked my father to take him and get him stuffed for me. I had the idea that someone at the health station where he worked must know about taxidermy, since in the laboratory they had those hamsters and gurney pigs and white mice."

"Hmm. That's logical."

"I kept bugging him, so intensively, that at last he took the bird in his bag and said he'd see what could be done."

"How did it turn out?"

"That's where it ought to end. With me happy, preparing a little cage with a perch for my bullfinch. It only gets worse from there on."

"I guess he tossed it in a dustbin, and you had to come to terms with it."

"You don't know my father," Michal responded, puckering his lips a bit.

"Sure I do. Maybe even better than you do," said Věra without skipping a beat.

"Maybe that's right. Because I know him so well, in the end maybe I don't know who he is at all."

"The same thing's happening with us, little by little, don't you think?" Věra took off her glasses and carefully cleaned them of the drops of condensed mist.

If there's something that needs cleaning here, it's not her glasses, Michal said to himself in sudden anguish at the thought that he really might be ceasing to know who that woman really was who came alive in his hands some six years before. In his hands, although she had been alive for a good twenty years before that, all by herself.

"So what did he do with that bird of yours?"

"A week passed, and I was in constant torment, because I was so afraid that the bird really had ended up, as you put it, in the dustbin. He was gone, and I simply couldn't imagine that he still existed, somewhere. Then my father brought home a strange box wrapped in paper. 'Here you go,' he said, undoing the parcel. It was a glass box, and inside, against a dark base, was set a bird's skeleton."

"A skeleton?" Věra repeated, amused.

"A skeleton. A skull with a dull beak, spine, thorax with a large breastbone, the so-called carina, little legs with claws, and on its wings there remained some long black feathers. It looked something like a prehistoric archaeopteryx. They had removed the soft parts with some sort of acid. My father began explaining to me the principles of how a bird's body functions, placing special emphasis on the strong, convex sternum, which is built that stoutly so that the strong muscles needed for flight might be supported by it," said Michal, thumping his own breastbone reflexively.

"Do you still have it?"

"I think it was lost somehow, like all the treasures of childhood. But all the same, that archaeopteryx had nothing in common with my bullfinch whatsoever."

"Sure it did. The skeleton was the same," Věra said, bringing the matter to a close.

The steel cable hitched onto the seat of the lift and took it up into the air. They began to descend the Vrátna Valley[28] and with each metre they progressed, the area around them tapered ever more. The mountains at which, just a few minutes before, they had gazed from above, now towered higher and higher above them.

Suddenly it seemed to Věra that that was the way it should be. A proper strategy, to climb up to the top on one's own strength, and then let yourself be carried back down. She fixed her eyes on the cable cutting through the sky, and the sight pleased her. It could break, but it won't. She rested her head against Michal's shoulder and it seemed to her that everything was suddenly in harmony with her fatigue, with her cattish reluctance to move as much as an eyelid. The booming wind and Michal's words joined together in one quite amiable current, which lulled her peacefully. The occasional rocking of the gondola merely emphasised the contours of the small, necessary danger.

"If angels were to fly, really," Michal explained, more to himself than anyone else, "their skeletons would have to be constructed quite differently than we imagine."

If angels really were to fly, Věra thought to herself, *why would God have created birds with those frightful sternums of theirs, which push out of their chest like a mountain?*

---

28   A resort area of north-central Slovakia, in the Žilina region, bordering on the Czech Republic and Poland. It is famous for its skiing.

BOTTOMS UP

Vladek was no mountaineer, even though he lived alone in the cottage past Ostra Hora[29] that his grandfather built. His grandfather was a holy man; he left behind a coloured lithograph of the Most Sacred Heart of Jesus on the wall in the kitchen, unintelligible prayer books in a box in the sideboard, carpenter's tools, and a long heart-shaped shovel, the best sort for digging potatoes in the little sloping field in front of the cottage.

Granddad walked the seven kilometres into the village each Sunday to Mass, in a black suit with a hat on his head. That suit can still be found in the cabinet. Vladek wouldn't be able to squeeze himself into it, even if he tried. Narrow arms, short pant legs — what a small fellow he had been. When he thought of it from time to time, Vladek just couldn't understand how such small people (Grandma was a full head shorter than her husband) could bear so much work. And everything by hand — no chain-saw, no winch to pull the wood close. *Those were solid people. Unbelievable people*, their grandson thought, shaking his head. *Everything in good order, washed and swept clean, not like it is with me.* He waved his hand in that typical gesture, with which he always quickly tossed away the cigarette butt from his lips. Burnt his fingers again. *Well, that mountaineer frugality yet remained him. Smoke it to the very last bitter drag. But otherwise?*

Otherwise, his grandfather would be rolling in his grave, had he seen how he was taking care of the homestead. The planks of the flooring in the main room were as black as boot-leather; so was the eiderdown on the bed, from soot; a mechanical saw sat in pieces on the table, along with a bottle of oil, a bottle of vodka, ashtrays, tins, coffee mugs. Cobwebs on the walls, the window grey with dust, one pane of which he cleaned with his sleeve; this gave one a sort of view

---

29   There are two towns of this name in the Czech Republic — this is probably the one near the Polish border, in Moravia, in the Ostrava region.

to the wood pile and rusty machines that no one would ever fix. *Ought to cart it all off for scrap. But you'd pay the carter more than you'd get for the iron, so what the fuck, eh?* And another fag end hits the floor to be crushed out beneath a rubber boot.

Out back in the pen the sheep were bleating. *Have to drive them out to pasture. Draw the chain on the saw, toss the saw in the pack, pack a lunch and a thermos of tea, jump on the machine and off to the mountains, before the ranger's up. Seven hours, and the work is over. But first, first, a few ounces for the road.* He poured himself a glass of blackberry liqueur and went to drive out the sheep. *They can go by themselves; they know the road well by now. Just need to tether up old Kešula and the others will stick with her, Lidia, Zuzana and the two little ones.*

"All right, Zuzo, enough of that," he said, shoving away the greedy muzzle of the sheep, pushing at his pocket.

"It's there, it's there the apple, just wait a bit."

He watched the sheep munch the green apple while cleverly holding it in her expert lips.

Vladek was no mountaineer, all right. Otherwise he could not look on so calmly as the forest inexorably re-took the pasture land. Little alder shrubs, hornbeams, birches, here and there even a spruce. Just last year you couldn't see them for the grass, and now they're advancing across the meadows like the avant-garde of the high forest, which so terrifyingly bends over the glade that those unbelievably small people once tore away from it, and conquered with so much labour. *And so what? An invasion is an invasion. Same as those sheep you'll have to let go. They haven't been worth the effort for a long while now.*

"Get, get!" He gave Zuzana a fierce crack across her hindquarters, and she jumped away in fright.

Vladek was born in the new town of Havířov, which back in the fifties had sprouted on the meadows beneath the Bludovický Hillock. *One hundred thousand flats for miners. Flats like little cages. Living room, bedroom, kitchen, bathroom with warm water, what else does a person need? Self-serves and shops, a workers' cultural centre, taverns, hospitals, everything. Busses, dedicated links to and from work. Not like out somewhere in the hills, seven kilometres on foot to church. Everything at your fingertips, everything you need. Television, Programme I,*

Pogramme II — now there's fifty channels you can switch between without even getting out of bed.

He learned the electrician's trade at Bytostav. He was the one who pulled those kilometres, those tens of kilometres of wire though the new buildings. Fuse boxes, clocks, fuses, sockets, switches, lights — connect, test, and go. He passed through thousands of empty, bald flats in which young families would find their homes. He never found one himself. As he put it, it somehow didn't work out. It was something he couldn't even explain to himself. But it had to be something big, since it drove him as far as the cottage his grandfather built past Ostra Hora.

It would be a shame to let it fall into ruin, he would say to himself in excuse. *Waste of an inheritance. I'll shape it up and then we'll see.* At the start, he still travelled in to Bytostav. Winter and summer, thirty kilometres on his motor bike, and back, every day. In winter time, the last five on foot, leaving his machine down below at an acquaintance's in the village, and struggling up over the footpath cleared in the snow to the breadth of one shovel, from one lonely cottage to another — the way mountaineers helped themselves. Whenever he didn't go up, he stayed down below at the tavern, stuffed himself, slept at someone's place *and in the morning it all starts over and that's the way we live here.* Two pairs of long johns, wide army trousers, leather jacket, and off on the motorbike to work.

Later on, he tried something else. He gathered together some windows, doors, frames, coverings and isolation from Bytostav. He carted it all uphill, and in the rear portion of the broad-spread building he constructed an apartment. An apartment with everything, everywhere. A kitchen line, a toilet, a bathroom, shower, metal frames, glass doors, just like in a prefab. But once more nothing came of it. He never lived there. He just had it out back, for nothing, really. And again: cobwebs, beetles, earwigs behind the panelling. It got to where he preferred not even to go back there.

Then someone down in the tavern suggested that he rent it out to tourists. The kind that come to the mountains for fresh air. At first, he shook his head. *No, no, don't want to let strangers into the shed. Grandpa wouldn't be happy with that.* But then he met a couple who were interested. A guy and a girl, city folk, both from Ostrava. A beautiful girl — her hair a little reddish, but beautiful all the same, and the guy, he was a teacher. Vladek never really grasped it, where exactly it was that he taught, whether it was at a college prep[30] or whatever. Who cares anyway.

3,650, he said, ten crowns for each day of the year *take it or leave it. Last word.* The Ostravian paid half up front. When he explained to them that the kitchen line and the bath were not functional, and so they'd have to carry up water from the trough, they didn't utter a word in protest. *The main thing is that we have peace and quiet,* they said. *Yup, there'll be more than enough of that around here. No one comes around,* Vladek said, pouring out some of the rum they'd brought him. *You'll have so much quiet,* he said, *that* — he drew his index finger across his throat. The girl jerked back at that in fear. *Don't be afraid,* Vladek calmed her. *It's safe here.* And he poured himself another glass. And then one more for the other leg.

And thus the pair from Ostrava took up residence up there. The girl swept and washed the floors, the walls, the windows. They brought only a few things with them, nothing to speak of. As if they didn't have much in the first place. A cooker, a kettle, a pot, two dishes, a couple of books and a couple of blankets. *They don't even have a radio, the comrade educators,* Vladek said to himself, when in their absence he had a glance at the way they decked out the place. *A real lover's nest.* But what's that to him? *They wanted a cell, they got a cell. At least they'll keep it up for me.* He tossed a butt on the floor and crushed it. *They'll be sweeping up anyway.*

"I'm telling you, that guy is going to murder us some day with a hatchet, just like Karamazov," Pavla said in the sudden quiet, which slowly grew, like a shy pause after the long and loud drunken litany, which penetrated the walls from Vladek's room.

"You're thinking of Raskolnikov, with that hatchet," Ivan, her friend, corrected her.

"Pssst — maybe he fell asleep," Pavla hissed, whispering (as if it were possible to wake a drunk from his deep slumber!)

"Tell me please, why would he murder us? He's a good man, kind," Ivan retorted, but he caught himself pricking his own ear in the direction of the lengthening pause, which began to fill the building.

---

30   In Czech: *na gymplu.*

"He's a loner, a bit of a freak. He talks to the sheep and the dog, and with that saw and motorbike, maybe it's turned him just a bit."

"I think it's turned him enough, since he curses out his motorbike with *Whore Whore Whore*."

"I cursed out my own motorbike once with *Whore Whore Whore*," laughed Ivan, "back when you didn't want to go with me."

"You had a motorbike once?"

"Just imagine. Rode it to work when I was a labourer at the waterworks."

"Before teaching?"

"Of course."

"When you were single," Pavla emphasised.

Ivan became quiet himself, sensing that something heavy was in the air.

"And I'm sure you told the same story to your wife and children, how you couldn't study, how hard it was to change your profession from manual labour."

"Please, Pavla — you know how difficult all that was."

"I don't. I never experienced such a thing."

"But you experienced something else."

"No, I've experienced nothing else, Ivan. When I look behind me, I see only darkness, a darkness in which some ghost is moving about, and that ghost is me."

Both of them became quiet. The wood crackled in the hearth. As a matter of fact, they didn't need a fire yet. They built one merely from embarrassment. Only to thaw that, which all week long they had to keep on ice. Pavla lay on the bed with the blanket pulled all the way up to her chin. Her cigarette stuck straight upwards like a nail with a glowing head.

"A ghost…" Ivan shook his head.

"There are ghosts here," Pavla interrupted. "Two weeks ago, remember how we quarrelled about that birthday?"

"Um-hmm."

"When I tried to go by myself."

"What does that mean 'tried to go?' Why didn't you say anything to me?"

"Come on, you know. But wait a bit, and I'll tell you something about those ghosts. I arrived on the evening train. I waited a bit yet in the restaurant at the station."

"Well, I can imagine it — the lonely lover at the station, while her boyfriend celebrates his birthday."

"Even so. I was terribly angry. Then I came up. I went along the shortcut, along that narrow path that arrives at last down by the trough. It was as dark as midnight. I was happy that I was able to find my bearings. Then I glanced toward the broad lumber road and I saw something moving from the direction of Vladek's cottage."

"Vladek?"

"No. Two white splotches darting through the darkness. At first I thought they were deer. Deer have this white splotch above their hooves…"

"No they don't."

"You're right… they don't. And what I saw was kind of high above the road. These splotches were moving in an erratic fashion, as if borne on the wind. And me, I'm standing behind a tree with my torch off, and I hear these sounds, like someone coughing and sobbing at the same time. And those white splotches were dancing round and round in the wind. Then whatever they were they came out onto the clearing, where the road exits the forest for a while. It's then I saw that it was a person, a woman. A big heavy one, 'from this neck of the woods' as they say At Emil's. A little long in the tooth."

"Božka."

"Yep, Božka, drunk, flailing about the woods, with both arms bandaged. And these bandages were shining before her face, as she wiped away tears. I didn't know what had happened. I had already gathered enough courage to go out on the path to help her, somehow — she looked horrible. And then up top, in the clearing, right where you can already see our own window, there appeared the silhouette of a man, as big as a bear."

"Vladek?"

"Vladek. He leapt out into the moonlight as silently as a demon and roared at the top of his voice, 'Scram, you whore!' after which he kept tossing every name you can imagine at her… *slut, cunt*, horrible! I don't know about Božka, but I spun around on my heels and took off downhill through the black forest, alongside the stream, and I didn't stop until I reached the station, and the night train home. So that was the apparition. And I swore that I'd never come back here."

"I'm sorry. This is all my fault."

"How can it be your fault? It's always you, you, never us. When you do something out of spite, it always comes back to bite you. The only thing I want to know is what was going on with those hands of Božka's."

"Again, I know. Vladek told me that they were having a party, with Emil and some other of those mountaineers."

"Perhaps a birthday," Pavla suggested acidly.

"Perhaps. And Božka was dancing, it seems, until she fell into the fire on her hands. Vladek had to take her to the emergency room on his bike, and because she couldn't hold onto anything with those burnt hands, they bound her to him with thong."

"Is it serious?"

"Burns, blisters, but she can move her fingers. Except she can't do anything now. Can't 'slog' as they say."

"Maybe she can't slog, but she can still make a man happy," Pavla said with a significant grin.

"You're a bad one, you are," Ivan whispered, bending near Pavla's face.

After a moment, she pushed him away, gingerly.

"Let's go outside, Ivan. Let's go for a walk. I'm suffocating in here."

They went out in front of the cottage with a bottle of wine and a pack of cigarettes. Vladek's room was dark, but the door was wide open. Out back, there was something going on among the sheep. *Just don't let it be the ram!* Ivan remembered Vladek telling him that he's still mating his sheep with a neighbour's ram. *He'll be ready for the knife soon, but he can still cover a ewe or two. He might not seem up to it,* Vladek stated with a crooked smile on his lips; *he's old, but he can still beat like a thunderstorm.*

Pavla went back inside. When she returned, she had a blanket thrown over her arm.

"Are you cold?"

"Not yet," she said, and laughed softly.

The mist was holding on in the valley like water in a lake. And from that lake the dull summits of the mountains heaved up toward the heavens glowing with billions of stars.

"All of this, and whatever else can be seen, from each of the farthest of these stars, is our homeland," said Ivan, embracing the heavens with a broad sweep of his arm.

"That's how you feel?" Pavla asked him. In the shadows beneath the great trunk in the midst of the bald hilltop, nothing shone but the whites of her eyes.

"Yes," hastened Ivan with his explanation, while his hands hastened to her breasts beneath her clothes.

"Whenever I look at all these stars," he whispered to her, "I say to myself, 'you and I are the same blood.'"

"What? Even you and I don't have the same blood."

Pavla slipped off the blanket and her naked shoulder became the horizon of the starry skies above Ivan's head. She touched his tongue with her own. In this they understood each other perfectly. But only for that moment, torn from the stream of time. When, burnt through once more by that which neither of them possesses when alone, they shrunk back into the nest among the glades, they felt again all those limitless vanities surrounding them.

From outside, the frame of the doors opening unto Vladek's room were black. The building itself was dead. Nothing moved, not even a blade of grass on the lawn rustled.

From within, of course, the frame of the doors leading outside were full of the bright night. Standing in the depths of the room, Vladek felt his heart squeeze with a quick palpitation. That happened to him sometimes. Someday it'll burst of a sudden, and they'll find him lying in the middle of the floor, cold, hatchet in hand, as if he had been trying to defend himself. As if he had wanted to go outside and kill someone else in his place. Or just hammer a few chips into the cold stove. Or chop everything into smithereens. His heart was beating like a hammer.

The Ostravian guy and his girl passed in front of the doors. Hand in hand. The girl had her hair loose. They went past, and it was quiet again. They went into his wretched flat in the back as quietly as polecats.

He threw the hatchet down onto the floor. That thump must have been heard throughout the house.

"Come on, come on, bottoms up," he said softly, and poured himself a glass of blackberry liqueur. It spread a warmth through his body. He felt the window of cold and dangerous sobriety sliding closed. He lay down on the bed just as he was. After a moment, he pushed off his rubber boots and pulled the eiderdown up over him. He smiled in

the dark and mumbled that everything was as it should be. He ran his
rough hand over his face. He smelt only tobacco, blackberry liqueur
and ashes.

In the morning, when the rays of sunlight flooded Vladek's house,
everything was somehow different. The gate to the pen was open.
Vladek probably forgot to close it, or maybe the ram battered it open,
yearning for his home pen after his afternoon jump. The sheep, which
he never led out to pasture, were running confusedly around the house,
entering the hall and the room through the open doors, knocking over
the bushel of apples and jostling one another. The dog was barking,
trying to force them out, but instead of that, he just drove them deeper
into the building.

The man of the house was awakened by the noise, but it was all the
same to him. He didn't kick the circus out of the cottage, as he would
have done before, he just snorted ironically.

"OK, OK…" he grumbled, weaving among the sheep in front of
the house, where he had a piss by the wild rose bush and cleared his
phlegm.

"Hey sheep, sheep, my little sheep," he repeated, strangely gay. "You
came to pay me a visit. And you!" he snarled at the dog, "you shut up!"

The dog curled his tail between his legs and went inside, offended.

"Sheep, my little sheep," Vladek gave the bitten-over apples a kick.

"There must be order. Order, you understand! I won't suffer any
mess here!"

"And today," he announced, as if enlightened by a sudden
inspiration, "it's Sunday, and we're gonna keep it holy. Fuck yes. Thou
shalt do no servile work," he intoned, like a pastor in church, as his
grandmother once taught him the Ten Commandments.

He carried his chair out onto the porch, and next to it he placed the
bushel with the remaining apples, and the bottle of blackberry liqueur.
He called out to the sheep, tossing them apples.

"One by one, one by one. There's enough for everybody."

And where is the couple from Ostrava? he suddenly thought. *Still
asleep?* He grabbed the bottle and two glasses and stared off toward
the back, toward the apartment. He was in a damned good humour
today. *We'll have a drink or two. And a chat. They're my renters, and I
hardly know them.*

He knocked at the door. Nobody opened. *Are they really still asleep?* He looked up at the sun. *Ten thirty, and so quiet. Jesus and Mary.* Suddenly, he was gripped with a horrid uncertainty concerning last night.

"What did I… Jesus and Mary, I don't want to see!"

Carefully, he opened the door to the apartment. Nobody, nowhere. *Thank God. I slept through it all.* Everything in order, the bed made, clean, as it should be.

Deep in thought, he walked about the building, and caught sight of them from afar, at the end of the pasture.

"Hey!" He called to them.

They turned around and waved to him in greeting.

"Bottoms up!" he yelled, lifting high the bottle of blackberry liqueur.

They waved at him again and disappeared into the forest.

GABRIELA

"Timi… what's your real name, after all? Tim — that's not a Czech name. It's some sort of diminutive, like Tom from Tomáš."

Gabriela was looking at him with such intensity, as if God only knows what depended on the answer to this question. She narrowed her eyelids and stuck out her chin in expectation of some fundamental question now being made plain to her. *Then she'll bend her head back, open her eyes wide and laugh.* Timik well knew this etude of hers, but he never knew how seriously she played it. He didn't really get these sharp girls, decisive and attentive to details. For example, the movement with which she brushed away that one disobedient strand from her forehead, which had somehow escaped from the firm knot of her dark hair. She knew how to do that.

"My full name is actually Timoteus."

"Wow, that's a name for you. Timothy in English. Timothy Leary."

"Well, I'm from a Protestant family on my father's side. They've always given their children biblical names. It could have turned out worse. Some of the more nutty of my relations have given names like Eliáš, Abigail, Lea… Gadeon."

"Those are beautiful names. What was that one you said? Abigail, Abi… I'd like that for myself. I'm from a long line of atheists, so I don't even know what those names mean. Eliáš for example, that was a prophet, right?"

"And Gabriel, he was an archangel," responded Tim.

"I heard that, but I don't know if my parents knew about it, when they gave me that name. I suppose it was fashionable at the time. Like bell-bottom jeans. I think that if they knew he was an archangel, they wouldn't have named me after him. They didn't believe in angels. They certainly weren't any sort of angels themselves. Nor are they now. You know how they speak of one another now? Disgusting."

"I don't."

"And you don't want to. Be happy, Timoteus, that your parents have always loved each other. They do, don't they?"

"These days, it's almost like a person would be embarrassed to say it," Tim said gravely.

"That's stupid!" Gabriela's voice rose to a near shout, and her eyes narrowed dangerously. "That's the most stupid thing I've ever heard."

"And I'm the biggest idiot that you've ever met," said Tim suddenly full of some sort of heaviness and fury, which he could not seem to avoid in her presence. Perhaps he envied that sharp charms of hers, which at the same time he so admired.

"No, you're not," she said in a soothing tone. "I'm not as young as you think."

But she was, she was uncomfortably young. She leaned against her almost-new bicycle just like that: in shorts and canvas tennis shoes without socks. Her arms were naked, and her shoulders; only her girlish breasts were half covered with the top of her yellow swimsuit. *Gábina*. Next to her Tim didn't look young at all. Actually, Tim didn't have a good relationship with his youth. At eighteen he already felt that his destiny was adulthood. Only important things mattered. He was never to sunbathe or exult in movement; never to dance and have fun at a party. Not him.

They mounted their bikes and rode on down the path toward the cemetery, between the dusty little homes behind the fences of which German Shepherds and other large dogs barked at them, their ferocious voices testifying to the real disposition of their masters: *It's not safe here,* at the outskirts of town, in an old colony lost amidst the aspen woods, among which rise the rusty remains of industrial buildings.

Tim was behind Gabriela. He was having a difficult time keeping up with the sharp tempo she set. He wondered if she also smelled that oversweet odour arising from the depths of the weedy vegetation, that honey-sweet death, which covers the whole area. Then the bushes gave way, and the path rose to the top of a round hill, upon which stood a crematorium, surrounded by the municipal cemetery.

Gabriela was on her way to tidy up the grave of her grandfather Čestmír. This was a ritual of hers, which she performed on the last Friday of every month. At the start of each new year, she took care to write GRAVE on each of those dates. And she visited the grave like clockwork, on foot or on her bike, on each date so marked, and would have done, as her grandfather might have said, even if it were raining hatchets.

When the weather was nice, she descended the hill afterwards and had a swim in the flooded gravel pit. No one encouraged her to make those visits. Not her mother, who'd rather not think about Grandpa, nor her father, who couldn't bear that entire family. If he said disgusting things about her mother, well, he couldn't even say her grandfather's name. It was Gábi herself who got stuck on the ritual, honouring the memory of Čestmír as if in spite of everyone else. Then, when she lay on her towel near the water, all wet, she felt a great calm, as if she had washed from her body a portion of the shame that clung to all those people, from whom she descended. Tim had no idea how much it meant, that she trusted him so, that she brought him along with her.

They got off their bikes at the cemetery gates.

"You want to go to the cemetery just like that?" Tim said in surprise, gazing at the drops of sweat shining on her shoulders.

"What do you mean 'just like that'?" she asked, uncomprehendingly.

"Like that… not, not fully dressed."

Tim had figured that she had a t-shirt or something in her knapsack. *I mean, to the cemetery in a bathing suit?* He had recoiled at the sudden thought of the dignified funerals of his antecedents, and the no less dignified visits to their graves on Sunday afternoons.

"You don't like me like this?" Again the narrowed eyes and the jutting chin.

"I like you a lot like that," he was able, finally, to say. He looked at her and suddenly recalled what they had been doing moments before. He would have greatly liked to take her in his arms. He would most have liked to make love to her right there, or at least to kiss her, between the cemetery gates and under the doleful eyes of the puffy statues. But she wanted an answer, and the answer was far from simple.

"It doesn't matter," he tried to say.

"It does matter. What were you thinking, when you said it?"

She wasn't outright angry, but precise. Incisive — it would have been easy to cut oneself on her sharp edge.

"I'm used to the sort of traditional idea, that one visits the cemetery in a suit and such."

"So run off for your suit. I'm going like this. Grandpa won't mind. He liked the ladies. You know how much he liked the ladies? Till his dying day. When he saw a cute woman's backside — you just can't imagine — and he would tell me, his granddaughter, about it. He tortured my grandmother to death. She drank herself numb. She got drunk upstairs in the bedroom, while he took his girls into the workshop outside. Any sort of female. Gypsies on the street for twenty crowns. And when he couldn't do it himself any more, he'd tell them these stories about goats…"

"He must've been some Cossack."

"Oh, that he was, man. That was his nature."

"So he wouldn't have anything against swimsuits at the cemetery?"

Gabriela wanted to say something, but then, suddenly, she clamped her mouth shut.

"You know something, Tim? You know, it would have bothered him. It would have driven him nuts! He couldn't bear to see naked flesh."

"Now I don't understand you at all."

"Hold on," said Gabriela, waving her hands at the height of her shoulders, as if she were conjuring an old memory. "One day, me and my sister were running about on the lawn at Grandpa's, naked. We were squirting water at each other from hoses or something. Little girls. And he yells at Mama: 'Put some clothes on them! Get them inside!' And that was the end of the visit, right then and there. He couldn't stop talking about women, but I never saw a picture of one in his house, you know, those hateful ones, the kind that truck drivers have in their cabs. He couldn't bear them."

"But why? That's like a contradiction."

"But it's not, it's not, Tim. It makes complete sense."

Gabriela bit her lower lip and hesitated whether to tell him or not.

"During the war, he had been in a concentration camp. In the worst of them. Birkenau."

"He was a Jew?"

"No, a Communist. And there, he was part of a Sonderkommando. You know what that was?"

"Not exactly."

"This was the group that cleaned the gas chambers. Simply put, they dragged out all those dead people and carted them off to the ovens. They were naked, obviously."

"That's horrible."

"It is. It's the reason why to his dying day he couldn't look at a naked body. When he had sex with a woman, she had to be dressed up. I heard my parents talking about it."

"What did he do after the war?"

"Everything and anything. Married Grandma and had Mama. But it was impossible to live with him. He was a roarer. He drank, he tossed away money that he didn't have, he hurt people. He thought the world owed him something. How many conflicts he had, how many court appearances! In the end, even his commie pals kicked him out of the Party. He destroyed Grandma. She lived out her life, paralysed, in an asylum. He chased all of us away."

"How?"

"He hated my Dad. Literally. He offended him whenever he could. He simply couldn't stand that his daughter was with him. He called him a dud, a boy, a fuckup. He couldn't bear it that someone who didn't undergo what he had experienced could mean something in the world."

"But you, you liked him, right?"

"Yeah. And he me, too. Only me. Couldn't bear my sister. I kept up with him, when he was abandoned by everyone else. He would always give me a sip of his moonshine — he didn't have money for any other kind of booze. Anyway, booze didn't help him, like it helped Grandma. He always said 'frost don't kill the nettles.' He constructed himself a distillery: coils, cooler, tubing — he explained it all to me. I bet I'd be able to make one today."

"We ought to try someday."

"We ought to. He kept that still on his kitchen table. He kept his fermenting bread and sugar in old pickle jars. Each day he made a quarter litre, and that's how he went on. He also had two dogs, horrid beasts — they must've bitten everybody who ever came near them. Him too, because when he got knackered, he'd go at them with a fury. I'm the only one they never bit. As if he ordered them not to."

They arrived at the grave, and Gabriela set about her work. Here and there she pulled up a weed growing from the white sand, swept at the border stones, wiped the slab with a rag, lit a votive candle even though it wasn't dark, and placed an artificial flower on the grave.

Timoteus was sitting on the edge of a neighbouring grave, lost in thought and breathless. Even though he wasn't doing anything, it seemed to him that he was witnessing something spiritual. On the graves round about there were angels, in stone and plaster — only above the grave of old Čestmír and his poor wife there hovered a real angel — and to top it all off, Gabriel.

The afternoon slid into evening. The great sun hung in the sky behind the hill like a strange fruit floating in a poisonous syrup. The nearby houses and shops were breathing heavily in the stifling hot twilight. That evening, Tim and Gábi arrived at the gravel pit late. Inevitability, which had hung in the air all day long, fell upon them in the alder woods beneath the cemetery. When at last they swam naked in the cool water, they washed themselves clean of their own new shame.

THE CEDAR AND THE HAMMER

"Who's going for a smoke?" the nurse called down the hallway of the psychiatric ward. Of all the patients who had been wandering about aimlessly after supper in the segregated area of the closed ward, only two men put up their hands.

One was Doctor Kraus, a biologist from the hospital laboratory, who had landed here again after a drinking spree that had lasted several months. This was his second time here, and he was full of self-reproach because of that. After his first stay, he went away with a kind of hope, and even something approaching expectation. Now, that world on the other side of these white walls appeared as something even more inhospitable than the wasteland that remained in his breast. Doctor Kraus looked forward to the cigarette in and of itself. He didn't want to smoke in order to think about anyone, or to enjoy a smoke at the thought that he might soon be sharing one somewhere else, with someone else. He wanted to smoke chiefly because it was allowed him.

The other smoker didn't bother with such matters. Pavel Červenka, whom everyone called Paloš, a true frequenter of the institution, was still a young man. A kid, really, with an old man's features prematurely marking his face; a kid who appears not to give a flip for the surrounding world, and who, if he must give it a thought, thinks that it really, really isn't worth anything at all.

On their way to the improvised smoking area in the rear, they met the chief resident of the ward. Everyone, including the nurses, acted as low ranking soldiers do, when an officer passes by.

"Mr. Kraus," the resident said, calling him aside. "Since you're going to have a smoke, try and exchange a few words with Mr. Červenka, will you?"

"About what, if I may ask?"

"About anything. Just a chat. It seems to me that he suffers from a lack of human contact, and despite that, he's quite an intelligent person."

"I'll give it a try," Doctor Kraus nodded, suddenly pleased with the task entrusted to him.

"To live in this shack, it's not much, but it's still better than to be like those homeless. Those silly bastards who thrust themselves before peoples' eyes on purpose, with those bags of theirs, and go about all broken and dirty on purpose, so that everyone should see how shitty they feel. That's what I could never understand, why a person would like be proud of it, that they're fucked up, lying around in front of people's feet. What's that supposed to say? *Oh, look at me, they'll sweep me into the gutter like any other garbage?* I already know that people are shits. I don't have to prove that to myself. I can be a real shit myself, when it comes, as they say, to the breaking of bread. Everybody's got to fucking take care of himself, and no child's cap with pompom or dirty rags ain't gonna win anybody any sympathy. So I just don't understand those bastards."

Paloš took an intensive drag on his cigarette, as if someone was about to tear it from his mouth. They were sitting together on a pile of mattresses covered with waxed canvas in the middle of an empty hall. They tapped their ash into a can. Stripped wires were hanging from the bare walls.

"They're going to fix this place up," Paloš interjected. "Everything's gonna be new."

"What's going to be here?" Kraus asked, pleased at the fact that the conversation was switching nicely to another topic.

"When they get done, it's gonna be an ER. Intensive care, you know? So when they bring you here in a delirium, or unconscious, they don't have to drag you through GP, but slide you right on in here."

"Did they ever bring you in like that, in a delirium?" asked Kraus, fixing his eyes on the dark red stains around Paloš's nose and eyes, and at the wounds on his chin, which were just now slowly healing. Involuntarily, he raked his fingers over his own face, on which drink had left no such marks.

"No. I came here myself. Just like that. Picked myself up, and came here myself. To hide, you know? I'd already had enough of it. I was in a horrible place. I was afraid that it would end real bad, that I'd kill somebody, or that somebody would kill me. Even the resident said that it was good that I came. I could have ended up somewhere completely else, in a completely different way."

"What was it exactly that happened?"

"It was a real fucked up day. After a fucked up week — a whole fucked up month. Sometimes it just doesn't work out. So we're living in this shack, like I told you. We have it in the woods behind the railroad — a caravan thing. We bought it for two thousand from this railroad guy I knew. They hauled it there, to that open area, by tractor, and so we're there. It was best for us when Dad was still alive, and Mama, of course. So we lived in this barrack, but then the owner tossed us out onto the street, for not paying rent. Before that we paid him. Dad had quite a good income, and Mama brought in a bit too; but we weren't working, me and my brothers Kájoš and Peťoš. We couldn't get the hang of it, you know, that fucking capitalism. You can't work, so you don't, right?Back under Husák I was in rehab, and today there's nothing like that any more. We had those welfare checks, you know? We could've had them, if we went to get them, but who wants to listen to that shit, anyhow, at the window? Then our sister helped us a bit. She was living with this Kašpar — that was his real name. Holy fuck! *Alois Kašpar*. Tragedy. They had a kid, and got some dole money on his behalf, and so we got through on a little bit of that. Now and then we went on work brigades, helping out, you know. I have a trade — I'm a fitter. Learned the trade at the vo-tech. Didn't finish school, but fuck with that, who needs it? I mean, who has time? You need to study, and the TV's going full blast, your brothers come over and say 'let's go get a beer,' and so you do. Beer's more fun than books. It helps if you know how to weld. I do; I did a bit of welding here and there. It's good money, only when you're drunk, you can't do too much welding. If I had the money, I'd buy myself a Swiss machine and open a shop. But, fuck it, what good is a shop to me? I'm some kind of entrepreneur? My brothers, you know, my own brothers would steal me blind and fence it all away. It's better to have nothing at all, like that St. Francis, as my grandma used to say. Then you can drink yourself blind and when they turn your pockets inside and out they won't find shit in 'em…"

Paloš gave out a loud laugh which ended in a coughing fit. *That's how it always is,* Kraus said to himself, *as if those poor mistreated lungs themselves knew that there was nothing to laugh at.*

"Time we were going back, no?" Paloš asked.

"No. We don't have to. There's still a lot of time."

"I know that the lady doctor told you to talk with me, so that I'd whine a bit for my own good. Therapy. So, I'll whine on to the end. That was the end of us in that shack, after our parents died, because the new owner was a sharp one, no fucking nonsense. He didn't argue with us, he just gobbled us up and shat us out. Comes up and says *you gotta go now; now your parents are gone, and you're not paying anything,* you know? He offered us money. Just sign this paper here about closing our affairs, and in exchange we get thirty dollars. At first we chased him away. For fuck's sake, this shack of ours is worth something, you know? But then, you know, that's money in hand. We started getting suspicious of one another. Almost killed each other out of fear that one of us would sign the papers in quiet and take all the dough for himself. So Kájoš, the oldest, said *Let's come to terms with that faggot.* Then we'd all go and move in with the sister and her kid and that Kašpar. So we signed. Then we went on a nice binge for a week, after which we went over to live with Kašpar in that house he had from his parents. That didn't last too long, either. We'd spent our last cents on that shack. The kid was sent to an orphanage, where it's probably best for him, and Kašpar disappeared, the dick."

A deep sadness came upon Doctor Kraus. He'd like to whine it all out himself, but he never was able to. What would he say anyway, with a story like his, *a vicious circle. First abstinence, then here a drink, there a drink, then binge, binge, and another fall. There's not much more to say about that.*

"And so he disappeared, the dick..." the doctor said, trying to pick up the thread of the conversation.

"Yeah. He made another baby somewhere with another cunt. Even sent us a postcard, the cretin. *Give my best to Evička.* Sure, asshole, we'll all go over to the orphanage to give your best to Evička, you idiot."

"Well, we've really strayed a bit, haven't we?"

"Strayed from the topic as they say, no? So then, the day I got here. Well, we had been nice and shitfaced since morning. But not me; I had myself a little box of red wine, and had a level area spreading out nicely all around me. If it was up to me, I'd just sit on my butt and listen to the radio. But Kájoš, my older brother, he took it in mind that we should dig up this cypress and sell it."

"A cypress tree?"

"I don't know, maybe a cedar, like Dad used to say, a cedar, when he planted it on Grandma's grave. An ornamental shrub. Nice and big by now: a metre, metre and a half tall. Growing in the graveyard, on Grandma's grave — and now Dad was lying there too. Mama no, because we kept her urn in the house with us; never got around to taking it over there. Kájoš had a buyer for the cedar — some prick with millions, for whom he worked at excavating from time to time. He'd built himself a house, a villa really, the kind that he'd have this driveway leading up to, and for which he was looking for these shrubs to plant alongside. I said to him, *Kájoš, he's gonna tell you to stick that cedar up your arse. He needs seedlings, and not a big fucking sow like that.* But he goes *No, no, a mature bush would be better, worth more, you clown.* And he says that this way we could kill two birds with one stone: dig up the bush, and bury Mama's urn. And Peťoš, the youngest one, well, he was pissed off about those manholes. I forgot about that. Anyway, you know, on the roads there near the hospital? Those whores were changing the iron manholes for concrete ones. And so Peťoš was going to steal those iron ones along with a chum of his who had a truck, and sell them for scrap. And *they could cram those concrete ones up their arses for all the good they'll be.* He was so pissed off, he was going to go and smash the new manholes *so those whores would see for once and for all that that's no solution.*"

"I was trying to do the same thing," sighed Doctor Kraus. "To show them plain and clear that there's no solution."

He called to mind one of his conversations with the chief doctor:

— *You know, a person needs a solution. He needs someone to be with, in good and in bad. Especially in the bad, you know, when everyone stands there looking at you as if you were a dead cow.*

— *I understand you quite well, Mr Kraus. But you also need to understand that a person needs to accept responsibility for his own actions, and not just wait for other people to help.*

— *Not even the people closest to one?*

— *Especially not them. It's not easy for me to say this, but that's been my personal experience too, and I'm a little bit younger than you are. The longer you allow yourself to lie there, the closer you come to giving yourself over into the hands of...*

— *The beasts!*

— OK, let's call them beasts. You'll see them quite clearly before you, when the time comes.

— What do they look like to you?

— To me? She laughed bitterly, this pretty, somewhat scrawny, dark woman. *They look just like normal people to me.* She twisted her lip a bit at the word "normal." *Normal beings, who want to pull themselves up and out of the reach of threats and pain. And when you yourself are that threat, that pain, well, they pull themselves away from you. Naturally.*

— But each person can be a pain and a threat to others.

— Look, we're no saviours here. All we're trying to do is to regulate somewhat your personalities, so that you don't constitute a danger to yourselves, or to other people. But you know, after all, when it eases up a bit for you, you'll see everything in a different light.

"So then, you think it all through?" said Paloš interrupting his thoughts.

"Yeah."

"This is a good system here. I whine, you think about whatever, but that's OK with me. So, we got to that cedar, right? Well, you can't imagine how long its roots are. And we didn't have a proper shovel now, just a cramp iron. It was evening, and you couldn't see shit. Well, we knackered ourselves but good. Those roots were fast under the stone edging like snakes. I tell you now, that grave didn't look too smooth when we were done. More like a crater after a grenade blast. And we were pricked all over from them needles. We also broke the cedar a bit, pulling it out of the ground. And all the while we were frightened that the cemetery keeper might show up and see us. That's to say, I was rather afraid he might come, for his sake, because my brothers were so pissed off, especially Peťoš, that he would've probably wiped him out. He was smart not to show up. I know that he was sitting there in his room at the lych-gate, but quiet as a fucking mouse. So we took the cedar and were off."

"And what about your mother's urn?" Kraus asked.

"Aha, Mama. Almost forgot. I returned and buried her in the hole left after we dug up the cedar. Then I stamped down the dirt, so that nobody'd notice there ever was a hole there in the first place.

"Then we went off to that moneybags. Me and Peťoš stayed behind at the building site, and Kájoš took the tree up and rang the bell. Out comes this guy with a Doberman on a leash. Then they started arguing, first *no, come back in the morning.* Then my brother chucks the bush at his feet. Here I thought that he was about to release the dog on him. Then he said *a hundred*, and my brother, he wants a thousand. The guy starts to call him a thief. And my brother starts hollering that everything he — the rich bastard — has put up has been from stolen stuff, which is true. Peťoš said that he's gonna fuck him up along with his mutt, who was barking even louder now. The lights started coming on in the neighbours' houses. In the end, Moneybags gives him four hundred, and we got out of there fast. Peťoš still found some time to swipe a hammer. A big sledge, ten kilos — you can believe him when he says it: he knows how much iron weighs by hefting it. He took it from a crate there, where the stonemasons keep their tools.

"Then we went to the tavern, and there we drank up that money in vodka. We don't usually drink vodka, maybe a shot, but then we were so knackered that we weren't thinking. Then we borrowed some more money by pawning the sledge, only that Peťoš needed it, so we stole it again from the bar, but the barkeep was drunk himself as well.

"Our sister came by with some guy, got drunk and started wailing about having her child in an orphanage, and I went and said it's probably better for him there. And then Peťoš tossed that guy of hers out of the tavern. He's so jealous of her. And she said that he was a dick, but that she had some dough from him, and we went and drank that up too. Vale of tears, man. Kájoš kept moaning about that cedar being worth at least two thousand, that he saw the same thing in a garden centre when they went there with the crew for some materials, two thousand for this kind of small shrub and ours, what Dad himself even planted, Daddy he said, what Daddy planted — and how many times he swatted his Daddy across his chops! And now it's Daddy this, Mama that, poor Daddy and Mama buried here… And then all of us are sobbing like crocodiles, crocodiles! So I've got a good varnish on, and I start feeling something else. I tell the barmaid that she's got a beautiful cunt and that I'll give it a proper hammering and she says she's not serving us any more, and so Kájoš goes up to lean on the counter and nearly gives the owner a proper drubbing. To top it all off, my sister comes up and whispers that she's afraid of Peťoš, that he keeps like stalking her. But I tell her that I'll protect her, but how, really, against Peťoš, who's a frightful thug, as you'll soon see. And so in the end I had enough of the whole fucking lot of them, that family of mine."

"That's what it's all about, family," Doctor Kraus said in a soft voice, nodding.

"Looks like you haven't had it much easier, Doc, and here you're a learned man, not like us, thoroughbred retards. Your woman toss you out with your things, or what? Tell me. Pardon, if I've touched a sore spot…"

"That's a good one," Kraus waved his hand.

"Maybe we should switch up, change roles, like the shrink says, since we're shovelling all this bullshit together. But it's helped me, of a sudden — they got this thought out, they do. It don't work when you crawl up inside. That don't work."

"You finish it up, rather," said the doctor, realising with horror that he didn't really know what he'd say. He had no story. It seemed like just after an accident, stunned, you don't know what you've broken, what wounds you have. You've just got this bag of jumbled rubbish on top of you, hanging off you, and you just feel that you can't bear it, but you have to. As if after the accident instead of bandages and stretchers, they tell you take yourself off and watch you don't get the car dirty. And here you're off to the bus and trying to stop up the blood oozing from your wounds so as not to stain the coats of the other passengers. *The normal passengers, normal people, who try to pull back out of the reach of pain, Madame Doctor.*

"So get it over with then!" he growled a little fiercely.

"Sure. It's all the same to me. So we leave the tavern. My sister still had a little money sewn up in her clothes — she's a top seamstress — and said that she'll buy us a half litre for home. *But Peťoš no, no, let's go for those manholes, we gotta show 'em that they're all wrong with those concrete ones.*

"So Kájoš goes off with our sister home and we go off for those manhole covers. Why the fuck didn't I go home myself — shit, to my bed, my radio, cigar; what else did I need? But we're such fucking gangsters, we get that from Dad, when he got his shit up, he'd be flinging bricks up to the fourth floor… well, that's an exaggeration, to the second, rather. But he was a good man. He went to work, to church. We're baptised, all of us. You're baptised, Doctor?"

"I think so."

"Well and even so, it didn't help us much, did it?"

"Baptism doesn't make a person a saint."

"You're right there. We're no saints. We started up by the hospital and worked our way down the street, one after the other, each of them manhole covers shattering beautifully at the second swipe."

"And you never considered that someone might fall into one of those open holes and break his leg?"

"If so, the idiot ought to have watched his step, no? And anyway, there's a hospital right around the corner, where they can plaster him up."

"You've got an answer for everything, don't you?"

"If I didn't, I wouldn't be here. Just like then. Peťoš was in action. He's smashing near a parked car, and that's not going to please the owner. Somebody called the cops. I knew it wasn't going to go too well. I was lucky enough to get that sledge away from Peťoš, otherwise those cops might've come out the worse for it all. They'd've been handing over flags folded in triangles to the little widows like in that American film, what's it called, *Saving Private Ryan,* it doesn't matter, he fell in defence of the fatherland, etc. So I threw that *corpus delicti* over the fence into the hospital grounds, and when I saw that they're giving my brother a thrashing, I took to my heels and that was all she wrote. He's gonna do some serious time now, he was on parole. At least my sister'll have some peace — he really was breathing down her neck. And so, I guess this way I really did protect her."

"All right, and what else?"

"And so I went to the gate, over the fence here at the hospital. There I lay down: it was the only place where they couldn't blame me for anything. I lay there like a plank. It wasn't hard for me to do, because I was really, completely destroyed. So they carried me off to the ER, took the blood-levels which were off the charts and that's that. Here I am, in the warm."

"So that's how you did it. Success."

"What else was I to do?"

"I think that Pavel, in his own way, is quite all right," Kraus told the chief physician, when she visited him in his room later that night.

"In essence, you're correct," she responded carefully. "Now you've just got to find your own way yourself."

THE BOY

"And so it's to Vítkovice," Hans sighed in answer to the announcement, that because of a disruption along the tracks, the train was ending its course at a peripheral station.

"What's that look like, a disruption on the tracks?" asked Hans' fifteen-year-old son, his boy, so to speak. A boy who stretches up it seems by decimetres at a time, for whom his father's shoes are too small already, as was proven when, soaked through on a mountain ramble, he was offered his father's spare tennis shoes. He couldn't squeeze them on.

"A disruption…" Hans imagined the two bright, sharp railroad tracks lit up by the front headlamps of the locomotive. On it races and races until, suddenly, they end, and the machine breaks down in the black smut of darkness.

"…I don't know. Some sort of failure on the tracks, I guess. A bad switch, a derailed train. Something's happened, so they've got to send us round, to Vítkovice. I haven't been there for ten years."

"I've never been there at all," the boy added.

The train rumbled over the metal bridge that stretched across the river — a sign that they'd already left the Beskid mountains far behind them. So much for picture postcards.

It was just here that, way back when, we walked the slope of the mountains between the trunks of the fallen trees. Alone in that cold, with the furious mountain stream pounding and scraping at the flags of slate. No real current there, but tens of little rills branched into hundreds of smaller tributaries, which literally drop by drop spill out of the rock, there in the silence of the peak. Actually there's no silence there at all. It's just that a person stops for a moment, as if he'd actually attained something. The region spread out at the foot of the mountains like a dirty tablecloth, or rather a frayed and soiled map, with its stains of towns. There, see, there we'll live someday.

There we are now. The lights of the cottages at the lip of the woods remained in their places, just like the villages winking at the night with the red lights of unprotected crossings. We're just riding past large and motionless grounds with formidable mechanisms, and on though the Ostravice river to Vítkovice. No sense now in remembering all those returns, the cosiness of the patient homesteads; they're there just like your childish hand, which at one time I could hide entirely in my own.

They got out at the stop, which at one time was to be the main station for the steel town. Silent testimony to this noble intent is provided even today by the empty, wide-spreading hall with its broad staircases, on which a few pairs of the diverted passengers were shivering like the belated shades of those who built them long ago. Only one of the fifty lights hanging from the high vault was lit, and only one ticket booth, of a whole row of them, was open. Three drunks were swaying near the buffet. An attempt to buy tram tickets at the booth offering alcohol and dirty magazines. *Nope. They don't carry them. And it seemed as if the dust-covered, full-figured girlies on the magazine covers had no effect on the boy. Didn't even notice them. In my day, our eyes would fall on them a bit differently.*

At the stop in front of the train station they found out that the one tram that comes this way won't be by for another half hour. *What now?* Hans stood there on his tired legs and suddenly didn't know how to begin. *What to do with it all. What to do with the boy?*

"Let's just walk," the boy suggested, looking around the dismal surroundings with interest.

"You haven't had enough of walking yet?"

"I rested on the train."

He's still a child. All he needs is a half hour, an hour, while for us, it sometimes seems that the rest of our life wouldn't be enough. The remains of life. Ugly words. You imagine a half chewed piece of bread, that even kids wouldn't want. Give them rather a fresh bit, or even something without bread, some kind of bar, something in a shiny packet — how many of them inundate the world. The world is covered in the shiny sticky packets left after sweets.

They went down the street along the fence leading to the darkness beneath the massive bridges in the distance. *Can that hole in the fence still be here, through which we always passed?* thought Hans. *What hole — it was a whole section of the fence knocked down, rather.* They went down to the tracks just as a freight train was rushing through the signals with a clatter. They had to wait a while in the loud darkness.

"Fifty-five, fifty-six… fifty-six wagons," the boy counted.

They passed through the rail yard, and then through another hole in the far fence, which led to a development of low-storeyed workers' houses. From behind the fences, guard dogs took up a furious barking. Most of them were German Shepherds.

"I wouldn't have imagined that anyone still lives here," the boy said in surprise, curiously looking at the lights shining dully in the depths of the low houses. Suddenly, it seemed to Hans that he was looking at himself from twenty-five years ago. It even seemed to him back then, a kid from the housing estates, that this place was an island of sorts, transported here from another world.

Beyond the theatrical, thatched roofs of the colony there rose higher, middle-class homes of red brick. *Those were put up in the Rotschild years. Solid honest buildings, as you can see from the decorative friezes above the bay windows. Homes for the better sort of people, before the whole quarter was enclosed by the factory from one side, the expressway from the other, and finally the railway. It's become a periphery in the very heart of the city.* Lights were still on in a few windows; other windows were boarded up with plywood and planks.

"I used to like to walk over these bridges," Hans said, pointing at the pillars of the expressway flyover, which straddled the old quarter. "I'd look into the windows and see how the people lived there. Once I saw a young gypsy mother putting a child to sleep. It was just a moment, before the light went out in the room. I see it still today, like a photograph. This pink and red place and in it, a dark-skinned woman and a child among the eiderdowns. You couldn't see the child, but you felt it there nonetheless beneath the mother's hands, stroking its head. If I were a painter…"

Hans and his son were standing at the base of a tall cement pillar, as if waiting for something. *If I were a painter,* Hans finished the thought in his head, *I'd paint only her hands. If I were a child, I'd feel that hand above me. If I were a mother, that's how I'd stroke my child.*

A man can't be a mother. A man doesn't dare enter a red and pink room. He can only lean on the railing and peek inside. Hide his hands behind his back, dig his nails into his palms, wipe the tears from his eyes.

Hans looked into the face of the boy. His eyes were impenetrable. He couldn't look into them as he did before, when that small child's head lifted itself up toward him trustfully from the pillow.

In silence, they walked on down a few more streets until they came to a square, from which some trams heading their way would depart. *We'll be home in just a bit. But before that, before then, we'll still stop here for a coffee.* Hans wanted something to hold on to; he wanted to prolong this excursion with his son just a bit longer, this excursion, which was now coming to an end. They went into a large restaurant with long, empty tables. There were only a few silent people there, some sullen men, a sore, drunken woman and a few desperadoes, seeking wealth at the gambling machines.

"No chance of that happening," Hans explained to his son. "They're rigged to take money, not dispense it."

Maybe he shouldn't have brought his boy into a place like this. But then again, he wasn't a child any more.

They bought beer and lemonade. For a moment, they seemed to be in the waiting room of a train station, at which trains no longer arrive. Then his boy asked,

"Dad, you used to live around here?"

"Rather, I worked and…" He began to tell his son about his life in the last century. About the workers' changing rooms, the cadre questionnaires, the Communists and accidents at work.

Again he smelt the stench: sweat, oil, and something else yet, a kind of dirt that reeks like burnt gloves that you've been plunging in God knows what. You smelt it everywhere, like when you scorch a fan belt. There was no escape from it: neither to an office, nor a university, nor Prague itself. You can still smell it when you open the pages of the newspapers from back then.

The beer and the lemonade were soon gone. They had to leave. He held the door for the boy, who went out first. He felt that his son was still uncertain in his body: he swayed like a beanstalk. And soon he's going to have to push him away and remain on the periphery by himself, those outskirts that appeared in the centre of his own heart.

TRICERATOPS

It was a problem, after all. How to arrange a bottle of wine and four pastries in the satchel, in which Jaromír otherwise carried only croissants and tins of pâté, along with his journal, his books and the news… They could be jammed in, sure, but it would be nice not to destroy those pastries before he got home. Idiocy. He could just carry them in his hands, as they are, wrapped in paper, but he couldn't see himself doing it, walking along the estate with a fluffy package. *Might as well carry a nosegay.* This was probably the main reason why he never bought flowers. For his own place, of course not, but not for others either… He'd have rather solved the whole thing with a box of chocolates, like in that joke about the policemen at the funeral. *Nosegays and fluffy packages? No, no.* A real guy has only one, compact little satchel, best if it's a leather one on a strap, and what can't fit in it is superfluous.

He'd quite like to toss all these damned cream puffs into the first ashcan he passed. He was in dread of them, with the strange brittleness of their shells frosted with sugar, and inside — *ugh —* their white mass of whipped cream and beneath them, another pudding cream — sticky and gooey like the secret innards of some sort of clam. *What the fuck am I doing with this crap? I'll get myself properly mucked up and sticky from these goodies. She says 'bring home some pastries' and I, idiot that I am, stuff this nonsense into my bag. And who knows if they're any good, anyway. We never ate them at home, and later, even later I never bought them, until now. But that woman says…*

Jaromír's inner voice grew quiet. It was replaced with the image of that girl Lenka standing in the doorframe of his apartment on the eleventh floor. Loose flowing clothes with a flowery pattern, low-cut, revealing her chest, those beautiful round breasts of hers lifting up; her broad forehead with eyebrows bending high above her dark eyes, made even a little larger by her strong, frameless glasses; her half-opened mouth and her chin, which is simply second to none.… No woman ever came to him like that. Or ever sent him out for wine and pastries.

No woman — in the vacuum of that conjunction of words he lived through years and years of returning home from work alone. Coffee, a croissant with pâté, then a cigarette, everything safely arranged around the book, which he wouldn't be reading for the first time.

That vacuum couldn't be filled by those several awkward attempts, when he was at a party at a friend's house — a friend of whose friendship he had reasonable doubts — and he stumbled against some girl (since they were all drunk) and led her somewhere by the hand. It could never be filled by that fucked-up slut Alena, obsessed by the fact that the better sort of fellow never has a taste for her; once she cornered him on the floor in his chum's foyer and jumped him. It was savage and sweet, but bad, corrupt. Corrupted by the knowledge that everyone knew about it, and kind of jovially were wishing him well with it, the cripple, who was ready even before that ardent Alena caught her breath, then just sufferingly agitated between her arms and legs like some sort of violated child.

No woman, he said to himself again and again. He preferred to avoid the places where something similar might chance to happen. And now, that girl Lenka was waiting for him at his own place, and he stuffs these torts into his satchel and his hands are trembling, as if he had touched something quite different from pastries.

He left the store. Oblique rays of sunlight slanted against the walls of the prefab buildings. Here and there, windows were completely washed over by the coppery light. They shone like the bronze shields of warriors. This will be the angle that will bind the vector of my sight to the vector of the sunrays. He imagined a simple sketch. *If I looked at my own window from the right angle, it would be ablaze just the same. But I'd have to spend a lot of time searching for the right position. Searching for the position. Oh God.* His knees buckled at the thought of that quite unknown quantity named Lenka in the bronze light that suddenly flooded his one room.

"You've gotta calm down a bit, Mirku," he said to himself in the whisper in which he often addressed himself. He took a circular route by way of the overgrown intersection of the development and the neglected fields, the wild deciduous forests. He gazed at the rough landscape with its villages, which the city will swallow up in no time, and, as always, every detail troubled and exasperated him — symptoms of civilisation. Jaromír loved the canvasses of Zdeněk Burian, which he knew from books about prehistory. Their content and form were as clear as a well-grounded paleontological hypothesis. The landscape of the Upper Permian. The Carboniferous ur-forests. The Oceanic Shelf of the Later Cambrian. Flora and fauna as pure examples of their types in the natural biotope. Sediments and volcanic formations and climates representing comprehensible conditions for the development of life. *No confusion, churches, towers, houses, trains.*[31] *What about all of this?*

What shall we say of man, who commits all this mischief on the landscape? Each day he meets people on the bus who are so different from one other, that it's like they don't belong to the same species. How safe and unequivocal in comparison with them seems Burian's picture of a Neanderthal, leaning on his club in front of his cave, or the Cro-Magnon in his clothes of skin, with bow and arrows in his already perfectly human hands, a little subtle in comparison with the clumsy upper limbs of that Neanderthal even, or the Australopithecus — *there's really no comparison there at all.*

Jaromír glanced down at his hand, bearing with exaggerated care the satchel with its delicate contents, and felt a sudden desire to throw it far away from himself. But he just gripped the handle more firmly and walked on towards that apartment tower, where that incomprehensible woman, a stranger, actually, was waiting for him.

It was in Lenka's nature to be curious. *A quizzical creature,* as her father said, when he caught her rummaging about in his things. It was curiosity that led her to Jaromír. He interested her from the moment she first caught sight of him, curled in a chair in the library of her friend Hans. The place was full of people who, bolstered with wine, were trying to drown each other's voices out in a discussion concerning what is, and what is not, modern art. Jaromír, Hans' friend since childhood, didn't even seem to notice them. He was taking down book after book, glancing at them cursorily, and then placing

---

31   In Czech, these words are given in a series of diminutives, as if a child were speaking: *kostelíčky, věžičky, domečky, vláčky.*

them back. It seemed to Lenka as if he were doing inventory (she had worked as a librarian while at university). Finally, he set two books aside on a little table without even asking, in preparation to take them away from Hans' place. It seemed that this was *de rigueur* with them.

They got to talking. Lenka didn't try to understand Jaromír's somewhat convoluted explanations, why only these two books, from among the whole library, could interest him. She followed the undulations of his voice, their peculiar, passionate peaks, which that man — at least ten years older than she — tried to suppress, but then again gave free rein to in unguarded moments.

The unguarded blink of an eye — that's the proper term, Lenka said to herself, who in a childish way relied on her social intelligence. *If I want to get to know that fellow,* which, suddenly, she did, *I need to encounter him in the unguarded blink of an eye.*

And so she set up just such an unguarded moment. His flat was also unguarded at the time. She found therein a library, in which serious scholarly publications were mixed up with children's books. *Well, after all, why would he separate them out, since he's alone? When he has his own kids, logically, he'll put them in separate bookshelves. That only makes sense.*

She found windows that no one had washed for at least half a year. Unless it was the spring rain. A relatively clean kitchen; carpets, which are perhaps vacuumed from time to time. Practically nothing in the refrigerator. Laundry in the basket surprisingly clean: evened, but not ironed; tee shirts and tee shirts and on a hangar one rather touching suit and a dress shirt draped with a tie already made. With compassion, she sized up the moderately wide trouser bottoms, which again after ten years were making a comeback. Everywhere were strewn open packets of cigarettes, and malodorous ashtrays. On the wall hung a picture, the author of which seemed to have wished to return to the last century. In general it seemed to her that Hans' buddies didn't take this twenty-first century too seriously. *It's not that serious anyway.* She suddenly remembered the periodical *Cosmo Girl,* which recently she found in her younger neice's possession. "How to be 'in'?" *These guys, it seems, spent their time thinking of how to be "out."* She laughed, and thought, deep down, that this is probably why she liked them. She herself sometimes found herself between, and being between, her social intelligence warned her, won't do for too long.

Gingerly, she lay down on his bed. It had no scent — just a little, of tobacco — but it was quite the strange lair. *If something was going to happen, the carpet would be better,* she said to herself, surprised that she was counting on that eventuality. *And if he happens to be counting on her?*

Shaken by a sudden emotion, she went out onto the balcony. Balconies are the tower blocks' unsuccessful stabs at having a garden. She sat down on a bamboo chair and looked at the clouds, the bottom edges of which were coloured by the setting sun. Then she noticed a peculiar detail. The wall behind the balcony was covered with reed mats. There wasn't anything particularly strange about that, but the upper, uneven edge of the mats overlapped some sort of blue smudges, like brush strokes. She pulled the mat away from the wall. The little tacks in the thin surface of the plaster gave easily; it didn't even occur to her that she would have to reattach it. Maybe she didn't want to. There was a picture underneath. A kind of clumsy fresco done in tempera hues directly on the plaster. Sun rays, just as slant as those now warming her back, were falling upon an empty landscape. It was supposed to be a wilderness, it seemed. Greenish-blue stains in the distance, almost too substantially stuck into reddish sienna, represented lakes. *Water's not easy to paint.* The horizon was fringed with strangely conic mountains. In the foreground stood some strange trees and stumps and, deeper in the landscape, in the very middle really, stood a lizard. It didn't look much like a reptile there on its four, pillarlike legs, with its great head surrounded by a horned, boney fringe — standing there gazing grimly at the evaporating lakes, with its shadow lengthening in their direction.

He must have painted it on a day like this, Lenka said to herself in astonishment. She rolled up the reed mat and placed it in the corner. Then she went into the flat, took a moist rag and wiped the dusty tabletop, on which in a minute or so they would place wineglasses and pastries, and then listened breathlessly for his footsteps outside the door.

THE BURNING CHILD

The sky beyond the great curtainless widowpane was still entirely black, and yet it was morning already. This is the moment that the clock of night winds down to zero, and that of the day begins at one. Kateřina was able to imagine it. With her inner eye she saw the line of numbers, as if they were written on a blackboard in chalk, but there is no chalk, there is no blackboard. The digits hang in the air, there, where there is no air at all.

"Where are those numbers?" she had asked, when she was much smaller, and her parents drew them on the dust of the path with a stick.

"See: one and one makes two, and two and one make three, and three and one make four, and four and one make five," said Daddy, crossing through the row of vertical lines with a horizontal one. All she saw was a picket fence. She didn't understand what she was supposed to understand; she merely nodded so that she could get up from her crouch at last and continue on the path between the pines leading to the ruins on that hot summer day, which she still remembered chiefly as *back then*, when she still didn't know how to count. Somewhere in the back of her head she still preserved the image of her incomprehension, when she saw those lines or pebbles checked or crossed in front of her eyes as nothing more than lines or pebbles. In the same way, she remembered the incomprehensible shapes of the letters in their rows on the signs. They were not yet words and letters, but a mystery. Now at ten years old, she guarded these memories of her illiteracy and innumeracy like a treasure chest, containing her real childhood.

Perhaps it was no coincidence that her illness took hold of her at the same exact time that the numbers began to emerge from all those lines and pebbles. She didn't ask where they came from anymore. She saw them, completely differently, of course, from the world around her, but natural all the same in the flat world somewhere behind her eyes. She understood that the horizontal line that her father drew through those first four verticals can cross through all such verticals that anyone might draw. It was some sort of invisible ruler which, in contrast to the visible rulers at school, could be placed on anything — five hillocks on the horizon, five teeth in a comb, five swallows, and not only when they're sitting on a telephone wire like in the primer, but when they fly off, each in a different direction. The ruler flies off with them, transformed into a line that threads through them and says: five swallows.

Katka looked at the world, which had suddenly changed, and counted and counted. Soon she didn't have to count at all. She understood that the ruler and the thread in this invisible world, which is still and all closely intermeshed with the one we see, are stretched out taut, and that each step she takes has already been counted; each needle in the tufts of that beautiful pine wood has its own number, and when it falls to the ground, it is counted out of the number of the living, and counted into the number of the dead, which lie about the woods on the ground.

This suddenly became so clear to her that she preferred not to say anything about it to anyone. She thought that it was only she who knew of it. The others just go on stupidly shifting the coloured balls along the wires of the abacus, like they teach in school. Only she knew that this was unnecessary, that everything has already been counted up and that she could ride over these rows of numbers, large and small, as if on her bike.

Only she wasn't able to ride that bike, really. She suddenly became so weak, that she couldn't even raise her legs. She remained lying there as if weighed down by a log that she couldn't shift. Fortunately, there were other hands that could lift themselves, and her too: Daddy's and Mama's hands, as well as the hands of the nurses and doctors. Suddenly, she was living in the hospital, where they would place a thermometer under her armpit. This she came to understand as a perpendicular to Daddy's horizontal, and she knew as well that each gradation mark on the right may be assigned to another gradation mark on the left. And when those two points lengthen, always parallel to each other, there come about various great squares and rectangles, these kind of flat surfaces, which are transformed exactly, according to the manners in which those who ride over their reciprocally perpendicular roads change the length of the sides. People around her bed followed with fright the graphs running along the diagonals of these savage rectangles and coaxed the riders in her bloodstream to stop running about so wildly here and there, to slow down and resume their measured pace, like before. Like back in those far distant days when there were only lines and pebbles and no invisible world existed.

That's how Katka calculated the strikes of the hammers of time before sunrise.[32] That's how she arrived at the null point, which is just a hair in the series of numbers, but since it has no value, it can be separated out from the real numbers. She always had been suspicious of zero. The schoolteacher said that zero can't be divided, but it can be multiplied. That little circle signifying nothing is able to swallow the largest number as if it were really nothing. How many numbers have fallen into the abyss of that little circle? She saw it now like a ball of the thinnest thread in the world. So thin that its thickness cannot be measured even by the finest ruler in the whole invisible world. Even in that invisible world, that thread is itself invisible. If anyone found out how to divide zero, he'd find just a further invisible world, and in it, another, and another.

Katka laughed at the lip of the abyss, at which she now found herself. She wept, just a little, and only in her spirit, at the new mystery which added itself to the cemetery of mysteries located at the rear of her head.

It was still peculiar, but understandable now, that night in the hospital is horridly long. It's just a prolongation of the evening — a bad supper, after which the lady doctor comes around, smooths her hair with her hand and wishes her a good night, even though she knows that Katka is unable to sleep; then the nurse comes along asking if everything's all right, even though she knows that nothing will ever be right again; then the nurses and night staff have a long conversation in the examination room, like her parents used to do behind closed doors. Somewhere a television is playing; here and there someone goes to the lavatory and the conversations grow still. Dáša, the big fat nurse, sits herself down in a chair between the intensive care rooms so as to better hear if anything should happen, knitting a white sweater in order to have it ready for her grandson at Christmas. The lady doctor on night shift goes to lay down for a few hours in the doctors' room.

---

32   In Czech, the expression is more lyrical, almost punning: *Tak se Katka dopočítala rána ještě před ránem.*

Nobody says anything any more, but it's still just the prolongation of the evening. Even the pain that ticks in Katka's body is a kind of evening pain, quite good-natured, just as quiet as the green needles that fall to the white snow.

Katka watches attentively as the evening-night drips away and shrinks like the transparent IV sack, until there is nothing in it and they haven't yet broached a new one. Then, for a brief moment, it's like in the fairy tale about Sleeping Beauty. There's nothing.

And soon it's morning. Everything's different, unpleasant. The sky outside the window is still black, but now there are new staff about, cleaners. The lady doctor looks strange in her civilian clothes as she talks with her colleagues, who have not yet quite put on those white coats properly. Bedpan, breakfast (which Katka won't eat); medicines, injections, *Good Morning, Katuško!* and a fresh IV hanging from the rack, as full as the new, long day.

Why us? Why our little girl? Katka's father paused on the stairway landing. *A warm coat, a sweater, a scarf, and it's so hot in the overheated hospital.* He knew he had no right to the question. Incurable diseases simply must exist in the world, like children who die from them… But he must keep posing it, even though — and this is much worse — he felt how that question alienates them (that is, himself, his wife, and other children) from that little person on the bed of suffering. *When we ask a question like that, and we do ask it, then we're no longer with her; we want her different than she is now. We thrust before our own eyes the kitschy — I mean it — the kitschy image of a healthy child, like from an advert for fruit juice or cocoa. The golden body of health, to which each normal person has a perfect right, of which Katka has been deprived as if by some oversight, or perhaps she is that oversight herself?!*

Sweaty, stifled, overheated, he stood in the white stairwell, resolved not to move an inch until he should banish the thought, not just from his head, but from the whole world.

Things were lively that morning in the children's ward. With the Christmas holidays fast approaching, they were discharging everyone who could be discharged. All those cars in front of the hospital. All those anxious parents with warm children's coats, warm jackets, knit caps and gloves in hand. All those children's telephones, MP3 players, and magazines hurriedly packed into bags, and already out of the rooms and in the hallways. In front of the examination room, a queue of parents collecting medicines, prescriptions, release papers. And then their kids, into their happy embrace, and at last quickly, quickly off home to the Christmas tree.

Whole forests of them are already standing: silver, gold, violet. You can't squeeze any more gifts in through the doors; frantic teenagers with chain-saws and clubs are widening the windows as it were, so as once again to have a little more of life.

Katka's father stood by the white pipes of the central heating and hid himself in the memory of a drawing in an old children's magazine. Good boys were celebrating their boyish Christmas. They decorated a tree just as it stood in the forest beyond the city and set underneath it their boyish Christmas gifts. And suddenly — the gifts were gone. A tramp stole them, the orphan Tonda Pírko who slept in the near-by limeworks. The comic strip showed poor Tonda in his torn clothes running away with the brightly coloured packages in his arms to the darkness beneath real, undecorated trees.

Who cares that it ended well, that he returned the presents and the good boys found him a new home? Only that one picture, which wasn't included in the comic strip, that of the strange person with the stolen gifts in the black, frozen world of limeworks and children's hearths is real. *But we are we and our stories are more lifelike.*

He had to chuckle in his sorrow. It was a good laugh. In the mirror of the glass doors he saw his eyes and his lips, so similar to the eyes and lips of Katka, as he might have seen them, were he present at one of the few moments when she had to deposit, again, the next mystery into that little cemetery in the depths of her little head.

He threaded through the groups of happy parents and children and headed towards the rooms where 23 December changes nothing. His hand was already on the doorknob when he felt the hand of the chief physician of the children's ward fall on his arm.

"I hate to say it, but Katka's taken a turn for the worse. Her temperature's risen. She's quite fevered, and not quite herself."

"But we can go in to her? My wife is also on the way."

"Of course. For as long as you wish."

He entered the room and swallowed the phrase he had prepared: *Black knight to H3.* He always tried to play imaginary chess with his gifted child. While he had to prepare his moves ahead of time and learn them by heart, Katka always reacted on the fly. He always lost after the third move.

Today chess wouldn't be fitting. It seemed to him that the child lying before him attached to those many tubes was burning from the inside out. When he touched her, he felt that the same thing could be said about him.

He wasn't in a mood to talk, but the word came out by itself.

"Story?"

Katka nodded.

Outside the window, rain and snow were falling. It was quiet again in the ward, just like any other day. He told her her favourite story about the people that the evil emperor chased from their beautiful homes on the sea shore. They had to pass through dismal plains with herds of antelopes and wild horses, where they were threatened by cruel nomadic tribes, until they came to a halt far, far away at the foot of the northern mountains. There they saw snow for the first time, as it sifted from the black clouds above the rugged stone summits. They went on through a valley of tall spruces and firs, and from the darkness beneath the trees there padded out reindeer and elks, and the eyes of lynx and wolverines and snow leopards shone. Never before had they experienced such fright, and such beauty…

He had no idea if his daughter was hearing him or not. Her expression was concentrated, as if she were thinking hard on something, as if she were counting something again. How many horses, how many dogs, how many lances, how many axes, how many trees must be cut down in order to build a house, how many logs must be prepared for a long winter, how much dried meat…

"Go on," his wife urged him, having entered the room silently and taken a seat on the other side of Katka's bed.

"I don't know how it goes on from there," he admitted, honestly.

"It has to go on somehow."

"Daddy, how many numbers are there?" Katka suddenly asked him.

"All together? I don't know."

"Come on, how many?" her mother prodded him. "You've got to tell her!"

"There are an endless amount of numbers," he said, drawing a horizontal eight on the coverlet.

"What does that mean?"

"That means, that after every number in every row, there's still one more."

"And after that one, still one more," his daughter added.

"And so on," her father nodded.

The little girl smiled. Katka was calm now, because she understood that the one tiny hair's breadth of time, which still remained them, would be as long as all the other time in the world.

SALAMI HORSES

Roman was embarrassed. It wasn't because of that provocative woman serving in the refreshment stand, or her sun-tanned skin with the white stripes left by the straps that he supposed all that long sunny yesterday had kept up on her body the thin blouse, which girls today call a *top*. At work today, she had nothing on but the bikini bra of her swimsuit, which without any sort of straps miraculously held on to her large, somewhat sagging breasts; a trick that these women are expert at; a trick they have for the men and boys when they hand them warm bottles, bending over to pull them out of the chests beneath the counter, or when they stretch out all their curves to reach the button of the radio on the highest shelf behind the chocolates and cigarettes, turning up the volume with their green-painted, long-nailed fingers when their favourite hit comes on Radio Kiss. *It's a kind of a slow dance, by which that bored shop woman separates herself from the life she leads somewhere in some flat or little house with an open mortgage and a husband and children. If you just heard her gossiping with her friend or her neighbour, you'd be sick of it before she got to the part about money and cosmetics and brand-name duds for the kids; you'd be sick of that whining like a television trailer — but at least here, to the slow rhythm of the radio station, the name of which provides a sort of zest thanks to the thunderbolts of those two sharp S's, you suddenly see her multiplied with all of the fetching barmaids and waitresses, who offer more than just drinks.*

"Only men should serve drinks in taverns," Roman's mother always used to say. "Women don't belong in bars. No good girl can run among boys all day long and…" *Cut it out already,* Roman growled silently at his absent mother, in a way that he would never have permitted himself to do in her presence, and wrapped his large hand around the necks of two bottles, a *Kozel* for him and a *Kofola* for his son.[33]

---

33   *Kozel* is a Czech beer brewed in Velké Popovice; *Kofola* a cola-like soft drink.

He left a bigger tip than he had intended to, and returned to his son, who was the real reason for his embarrassment. He was sitting on the grass next to two bikes leaning together, staring at the waters of the river flowing by. *Robert.* His name was a compromise. His mother wanted to name him Roman — the first son should be named after his father. His wife wanted Norbert, after her father, who died when she was still small. And so it's Robert sitting there, whose name is mixed together just like his chromosomes.

"So then, Robi, everything OK? Your legs aren't hurting you?"

"Not yet."

It always seemed to him that his son answered kind of evasively. He always leaned his head toward his right shoulder, as if he wanted his father's words to pass by his ear over his left shoulder, and get lost somewhere in the vacuum.

"He doesn't like to look people in the eye. Up at the board, he always looks down at the floor and speaks so softly that you can hardly hear him. All the same, he nearly always has the correct answer." Thus sighed his teacher at the parents' conference for 6 B.

"He's sort of shy," explained Dr. Roman Hradílek, his eyes fixed on the pattern of the floor covering at the woman's feet. He too had some trouble looking people in the eye, especially women. Even during sex. *It's best from behind. Then a person is actually alone, and can experience it in his own way.* Through his head flitted his favourite image of an eerie, certainly Thai brothel, where the whores come to one naked already, walking backwards and never, in any case, ever dare to turn around and have a look at the man who is about to enter them, even if, even if… With difficulty, he chased from his head the shadowy room with its oriental hangings, in which a woman's back end appears, and disappears again when it's all over, when it's all, damn it, over.

When they finished their drinks, he sent Robert back with the empty bottles. Then they got on their bikes and resumed their ride along the river. The fresh morning air suddenly gave way to a thick mugginess. A heavy storm cloud was hanging over the green of the pastures and the woods of the floodplain. They passed some horses on their way. They were nibbling at the grass at the end of long chains attached to iron stakes driven deeply into the ground. From one of his trips, Roman remembered a dark skinned boy with sidecurls, wearing a black woolen cap on his head, even in this heat. He had an iron stick in his hand and was jabbering something at an apathetic animal, too small for a real horse and too big and robust for a pony or a donkey, a mule, or whatever else can be obtained from the interbreeding and bastardising of these poor perissodactyls. Three mares and one colt were at pasture here, and so crudely, as if they themselves intuited that their appearance must turn the stomach of any breeder or student of noble steeds, or even of honest, hardworking draught animals. Fiercely, they crushed the green grass with the resignation of cattle who know that, outside of fodder, nothing good is awaiting them in this life.

And yet. Little Robert, who was riding in front so as not to be left behind by his father's quicker pace, jumped from his bike, pulled up some dandelion leaves and approached a mare, the one who was as black as tar.

"Careful, Robi, you have to go around her," Roman called out. "She could strike out and kick you. Never approach a horse from the rear."

The boy heeded the words. He gave the powerful shanks of the mare a wide berth, and in a moment was gazing into her dark, shining eyes. From up close, they were so alive, as if they beheld at once the whole bloodsoaked world. With deft lips she took the leaves from his hand.

"Stroke her calmly, on her face, horses like that," his father advised him. "Like this, see?"

But Robert was shy. He just touched her lightly between her eyes and took a step back.

"What kind of horse is she?" he asked after they had ridden along awhile again, and reached a place where the road widened so that they could ride alongside one another.

"Those are… You know, I call them salami horses."

"What do you mean, salami?"

"They're the sort of nags that no one rides, or even hitches up to pull things. They breed them for meat. When they're grown, they sell them to the knackers."

"You mean some people eat horses?"

"Well, sure. There's horsemeat salami, cabanos — real cabanos is made from horsemeat or donkeys. When I was in Belgium, I saw a whole herd of horses at pasture, just like cows, behind electric fences."

Robert pumped at his pedals, so as to pass his father by. He pushed at them like a madman, until it became dangerous because of the uneven road. *That's all him*, Roman thought to himself as he let him go on. *He's his mother's son. It's like watching Uršula. If she came out on a ride with us, if she wasn't just lying round at home and complaining about her headaches, while I, a doctor, know better, don't I, that she's perfectly ok… If she wanted to get on a bike too, she'd run away from everything I said, just like Robert now. Head over heels, up and away. Wherever: into a pit, across the rails, under the train itself, wrong way right at a lorry without the blink of an eye — let it break me, let it kill me… And then you go on, go on if you like and bear it, what you've made of me, you vile, untruthful bastard!*

The road narrowed to a pathway leading into the midst of the riverside forest. Huge trees: lindens, alders, maples, oaks and innumerable hornbeams enclosed them in a balmy twilight. The path twisted and turned in the thick undergrowth of bear garlic, the white flowers of which twinkled like sparks. They had to slow down as the path descended into the vale that remained here among the old dry arroyos overgrown with nettles and bedstraw, and then ran again uphill to the actual riverbanks. It would have been easier to dismount and push the bikes along, but it is the lot of riders on mountain bikes with their deeply patterned barrier jackets to stay in the saddle and foolishly strain the steel tendons of their sophisticated gear wheels.

They also had to bob and weave around the many snails which, in their infallible premonition of coming rain, had crawled out onto the path. *Why are you so afraid of that crunching, and the slimy seepage on the crushed little house? You're so afraid that you'd rather jam on the breaks and tumble into the nettles…*

"Let's go on foot from here," Roman decided, and noticed that Robert was more than happy to agree.

When they dismounted, they saw that the sky looked rather threatening. The bit of the heavens that they could glimpse between the crowns of the trees was a livid darkness, and the sharp saw of the rain began to tear into the thatches of young spring leaves high aloft. They hastened their tread, even though Roman knew that there was no shelter for quite a few kilometres. *Senseless.* And the treetops let the rain through. In a minute, they'd be soaked to the skin. His money, documents and their telephones were safe inside the old knapsack of waxed canvas. One thunderclap boomed, and then another. Two bolts of lightning like those in the word "kiss" crackled between heaven and earth. Another one, and now the thunder sounded behind them. It had grown as dark as night. At first they still sought out the trees with the thickest crowns, but then they just stood there helplessly at an intersection of wooded paths. They half-sat on their bikes, like a pair of strange, tall animals.

"We have to wait it out," Roman said to his son. Both of them watched while the torrents of water began to churn the forest floor into a swamp. The boy quietly leaned against his father's side. You could hear his breathing. Both of them looked down to the mud at their feet. There was no longer any dry place on which to stand.

Then they heard a strange crackling in the treetops, as if something were tearing the leaves from the branches. Hail. Sharp, angular pieces of ice began to strike the path, crashing from the clouds to the earth in a blinding white flood. The boy's hands flew to his head, and he cried out in pain. Roman crouched over him, shielding him from the pellets with his broad back. Almost blindly, he reached out with his hand for the knapsack fixed to the bicycle frame. As he was undoing the straps, the hailstones battered his knuckles like little hammers. It hurt like hell, but at the same time was pleasant. The boy was shivering beneath him like a lamb beneath a ewe. Roman undid the pack and placed it on his son's head and shoulders. Then he stood up straight and had a look about them. Bits and pieces of ice struck him about the temples and the crown of his head. He didn't try to shield himself at all, just intensively took in the pain, the cool of the ice and the acrid odour of the torn leaves and the crushed bear garlic. He pressed his hands to his brows, creating a little roof for his eyes, from beneath which he gazed at the furious elements of the storm, seized by a strange, delightful enthusiasm.

"Daddy, when will it stop?"

"In a minute, in a minute. Hailstorms never last long. Don't be afraid. I can't wait to tell Mama!"

That sentence pained him worse than all the hailstones thudding at his neck. *Mama.* Actually, at first he thought of his own Mama, back in the days when she was as old as he was now, and he, with eyes wide open, related his adventures to her. *Adventures! Do such things still exist? Is there any woman today still interested in adventure?* The hailstones rattled down like his enthusiasm. A moment more, and it was all over, including the rain. They pushed their bikes through the drifts of quickly melting ice as the first oblique rays of sunlight penetrated the forest.

After a few steps they found themselves on the shores of a lagoon, in one of the old blind arroyos. On the stone wall there stood a green shack with open, cracked doors. Not even one hundred metres from the place where they waited out the hailstorm! How cosy it would have been in there! Nearby stood a little stone bridge, a floodgate and a fragment of a worn canal that disappeared in the underbrush. *Here there was a little regulating station,* Roman said to himself, *a waterman's or fishkeeper's lodge. That shack kept the weather off his head, bad weather like what we had to bear in the forest just like a couple of deer.*

When they pushed their bikes on to the causeway of the railway that cut through the riparian woods, the sun was out shining again, and beating down an almost unnatural heat. *One storm is never enough,* Roman thought to himself, *something else is on the way.* He watched the steam rising off his wet clothes. Like two ghosts they clambered over the brown stones leading to the bridge over the Odra. In the distance beyond the bridge, the white towers of apartment blocks could be seen.

It almost seemed as if that girl had fallen from the heavens. She hadn't. It was just that she had been hidden from their view by the arc of the load-bearing structure of the bridge. Now she was standing in the metal framing, above the river. In her hand she held a tiny telephone, as if she had just finished a conversation. Her wide-bottomed trousers were soaked through with water; a wet, tight bodice encircled her birdlike breast and thin waist; her reddish hair fell down around her shoulders, and the silver circles of her earrings sparkled in the sun. She stared at them with green, widely spaced eyes as if they were the first people she'd come across in her life. She was seventeen, eighteen, no more than that. Those eyes, with their shining, wet lids, went burning through Roman, arousing in him an incomprehensible awkwardness.

The situation was clear enough: she was too young for Roman, too old for Robert.

He smiled a bitter smile. She thought that he was smiling at her, and she returned an astonished sort of smile. They walked past her over the metal plates of the bridge, and there, where the bridge debouches onto the road, they mounted their wet bikes.

"That was a beautiful girl," Roman said to his son. He regretted the words immediately. From the corner of his eye he noticed how his son leaned his head toward his right shoulder, allowing his father's words to pass by his ear over his left shoulder.

EDITA

When the phone rang, Vladimír wasn't sleeping. He was just lying in the dark, staring up at the ceiling, as it happens with people who aren't able to do anything else. He could still make the children their supper, give them a bath, put them to bed and begin to read them a fairy tale from the dark woods. He would have read even further, but both of them fell asleep. There was nothing else for him to do now but to grow silent and go off to the bedroom and lay there like a fallen tree.

He gazed at the dark ceiling with his tired eyes, and didn't know who he was. No, not a bit. A cold forehead and sweaty feet. He was full of anger at all that love; he'd have gladly sent the one and the other to the devil. He'd gladly have lived alone with his own, for Pete's sake, his own children somewhere far away, on the Falkland Islands even. And so he turns around and buries his head in the pillow, breathing shallowly like the most cowardly of creatures, who would crawl to any cross that anyone, even jestingly, should stick before him. He turned and turned in bed like a chicken on a spit, the mattress burning beneath him, as years of love never did.

Love. It was like a punch to the gut. That happened too, anyway. Not even a week ago. First they argued for a couple of hours and then his wife, Edita, took herself to him. He couldn't defend himself; it was as if his hands were tied. *Just no violence,* he said to himself, *never any violence that she could use against you in a court of law. When you get to the court of law. That court of law stacked against you, divorce court, where that female judge, three times divorced herself, will deprive you of your rights to your home, to your children, to everything. Well, not everything. Some human rights will still remain you. Just, no violence.*

You don't even dare to grab her by the hands when she uses them to slap your face, because your grip will leave marks on her arms. You don't dare put up your arm to ward the blow, lest she hurt her wrist against it. You don't dare push her away when she charges at you, breathing in your face and asking "How do you do it with her? Like this? Or like this?" and she touches you almost lovingly, definitely not mercifully.[34] *You don't dare to push her away, you don't dare to give it back to her, because she could trip and fall, hit her head, and die, even, if you poked her even once and screamed "how do you do it with that guy of yours?" Until you find yourself in court, in that court even more stacked than the other one, the court of morality. The only thing you can do is cringe in a corner, avoid her with your head shielded by your arms, when she tries to unbutton her shirt, pierce your skin with those sharp breasts, so as to make you do it; you don't dare do it, you don't dare rape her, you don't dare rape yourself, the only thing you can do is take a deep breath and be ashamed for your whole long life, be ashamed for her, what does it matter. What do we matter.*

She stood there stiffly and looked at him, as if she couldn't believe her eyes. Couldn't understand, that after all this action, as if by muscle memory he put on his shoes and jacket, reached around for his satchel, all the time looking fixedly at the red stain on her face and neck and making sure that they were from anger, that they didn't arise from any touch of his hand.

"Coward, shit…!" she offered him, when he slid past her like some kind of two dimensional being cut out of paper, along the wall towards the door. "You want to go, go!" she hissed, and struck him in the stomach with her little fist. She had it curled so tight that he didn't even feel it. "And don't come back!" The door slammed behind him, and he fumbled about the stairwell, all hot and panting as if after the worst fight of his life.

And yet he came back. He had to come back, until it was all settled. They have to swallow it together, they have to breathe the same heavy air of the apartment, in which two alienated people stumble around the beds of their children and with disgust bring up and spit out everything that they gave one another over these last ten years. Return it where? To the abyss, from which they first conjured it, with such labour? *That's the illusion right there, our pride. What on earth can be brought out of nothingness? Return it to love, which will go on now, without us.*

The ringing of the telephone made him jump out of bed so fast, that for the split second in which he was still able to think anything, it

---

34 The Czech original is almost a pun: *Dotýká se tě málem milostně, rozhodně ne milosrdně.*

seemed to him that he had jumped out right before it had even rung. And there it goes again, sounding so brutally and unmercifully in the quiet of the flat. *Don't they know that once is enough? Can't a person sleep?*

He picked up the receiver. Silence. Then a sound, as if someone were snuffling, and then it was Edita's voice:

"Come over here, please."

"Me? Why?"

"Don't ask, just come!"

"Where? What's going on?"

"I don't know."

"I don't even know where you are. You said you wouldn't be back before morning, anyway."

"Get over here, now," Edita insisted.

"Where is here?"

"To my office."

"Now? Do you know what time it is?"

"I don't know!" she moaned.

"Is something going on?"

"Yeah. Something."

"Are you all right?"

"No, I'm not all right!"

"OK, stay there where you are. And he… is he there with you?"

"Don't ask, just come."

"OK, OK, just listen, please, don't do anything stupid. I'm on my way."

Vladimír got dressed with mixed feelings. *She's going off with some strange guy; like some great boss, she goes out through the door, tossing over her shoulder, "Take care of your family," and now she's snuffling into the phone!* He searched out his keys, his jacket, his licence. *Maybe I should change my nightshirt? Who cares…* and he pulled the zipper of his jacket up to his chin, looked in on his children, and went out.

My wife is somewhere alone. That's all we needed. If that guy did something to her… If she, Edita… She's capable of anything.

Shit, what the hell am I doing? he asked himself, as he plunged the key into the ignition. *Am I some kind of idiot, some kind of Prince Myshkin?* But he was already rushing through the streets towards Edita's office. He was afraid that she'd do something. He knew her, the crazy girl, the hot-headed girl, who acts before she thinks. A wave of tenderness broke over him. He remembered how he used to glance at her, whenever her red dress flashed on the institute staircase. How out of himself he was, whenever he thought of her. He remembered that secret flat that they rented from that miserly old woman, that old pimp of a woman, who pretended that she knew exactly what they were about, and kept raising the rent from month to month. *Edita, we stood at the altar together. At least we could have left that altar out of it. But not us, no, before God and man. Before the whole universe if we could, like a constellation in the heavens — Theseus and Ariadne.*

When he drove up in front of the building in which the office of Edita's firm was located, a car which had been parked along the pavement turned its headlamps on. When Vladimír parked, the car drove off along the street somewhere into the darkness. Vladimír got out of his car and watched it go.

He opened the door of the building. He still had a key to Edita's office on his keychain. Once, not all that long ago, it had been his office too. And it still fit. He stopped at the door, and wasn't amused. He suddenly realised that he had underestimated the significance of why they had had to buy a couch, first of all, for the office, all those years ago. The timed light in the hallway went out. Vladimír didn't turn it back on. He tried to stick the key into the slot — something was already there, blocking it. Edita's key, probably. He knocked. Something moved inside the office. She approached the door. Her steps pattered oddly against the floor. He knocked again.

"Is that you, Karel?" The voice inside was broken with crying.

"It's me," answered Vladimír.

Even through the door he could sense her disappointment.

"You called for me to come, and I've come."

"And he… He's already gone?"

"Seems so. Somebody drove off a few minutes ago."

Vladimír was able to imagine Edita, leaning with her back against the door, unsure of what to do. Suddenly, he was helpless himself. So guiltily helpless.

"Edita."

"Hm?"

"Open the door."

She didn't even move.

"Open up. We'll go home."

"When I, when I don't even know what I'm supposed to do. I don't know! He's gone, he left me here and I don't know. I can't be with you, after all, Vladimír…"

"Of course you can. You can go home."

"And he left me here, and I can't go home. I can't go home, after all. Leave me alone! Everybody, leave me alone!" she screamed, and Vladimír listened to her steps as they slapped away again.

In for a long haul now, he said to himself. He sat down on the steps and lit a cigarette, like a husband who had been chucked out of his house. *Walk back up to the door and slam your fist at it like you mean it. Ha. Don't have the strength for that any more.* So he remained in the unstable safety of his perch.

It turned out that fist slams weren't needed anyway. After a little bit, the door opened, and Edita came out into the darkness like a shadow. She had her coat on, and a handbag in her hand.

"Hi," he greeted her in a near whisper.

"Vladimír, you're waiting for me here?" She took one shaky step towards him, and fell into his arms.

She let herself hang there, like a coat on a rack.

"I am completely lost. Understand? Completely lost," she whispered as they descended the stairs, he half carrying her.

"We both are," he said to her in a soft voice, settling her in the car. "But we don't have to go crazy all the same."

She pressed a handkerchief to her eyes and was silent. They drove off into the night.

"I don't know, I don't know at all what I'm supposed to do, what I'm doing, what will become of me. I don't want, I don't want…" she stuttered, until she fell asleep, finally, in the passenger seat.

Vladimír cruised about the streets, rather than heading straight home. They had time enough. That's one thing they had. He drove out onto the beltway and circled the city in a wide arc many kilometres long. On purpose, he drew out the ride through the peripheral suburbs and the nearby villages, where not a single light was shining in any of the cottages. He wanted to remember this moment, driving about like that all night long, because in the morning, in the morning everything would be quite different.

AND THE BIRDS AS WELL[35]

He preferred not to go outside because of them. He tried not to think of them. To chase them out of his head as if shooing them out of a dovecote. But they were always with him. He could avoid them only when he didn't think about them. But how to do that? The best way was to just sit there. The angle of his crossed legs securely wedged between the chair and the plane of the table. And then not to move a muscle. For a few minutes, long minutes, maybe hours. One knee resting upon the other like two human heads cuddling close. Flexing his instep and compressing the calf, until it began to hurt. He could tighten and relax that constriction. He could focus on that. He could think about the red spot, which was just now appearing on his left knee. He could do a whole lot of things. Balance his weight on his elbows and feel the pressure throughout his body. He could rest his chest on the tabletop and grip it between his knees and his ribs as if he were a pair of living pincers. Like the table clamp of a cast-iron meat or fruit grinder. *Such mechanisms function only when they are firmly tightened against the table-pad, the stability of which compensates for the vectors of torque of the functional elements of the mechanism. I, on the other hand, am a non-functioning mechanism*, Oldřich said to himself, with his head resting on the flat area of the table, *and I grip the table thus, only in order to feel something. But I can say the hell with it. I can lie down in bed, with a pile of pillows under my back, rest my heel against the frame and become immobile. Rest a bit.*

"Oldřich, Oldo, you've got to rest," he said to himself reassuringly, and glided from the table to his bed.

It was dark in the flat. He liked it best that way. The window was hung with curtains and thick drapes, so that one couldn't even imagine what was going on outside. And yet he knew, again, that they were

---

35   The title, "A ptáci taky," is borrowed from the text of a song by The Plastic People of the Universe (*author's note*).

 JAN BALABÁN

there. The sounds they made came to him through the two panes of glass and the two layers of fabric: sharp sounds, emphatic, like tiny thorns. Like leathery claws with sharp talons, the kind that puncture the delicate bark of the twigs of the apple tree. Oldřich couldn't help but hear the tiny cracking, the rattling, the rustling of feathers among the leaves. And quite somewhere else, in a different place in his brain, he simultaneously heard the quotidian noises of the house. Betyna opens and closes the door to the bathroom, to the pantry. The door of the refrigerator comes together with the frame, softly. Water from the tap, the clatter of dishes in the sink. The low singing of the vent, low singing from the radio. The daily humdrum sounds, and beneath them all, the scratching of talons and the rustling of feathers. *Maybe you can only hear it in this room,* Oldřich says to himself, all tense and pressed tight against the bed frame like a support. *Maybe over there, behind the wall, everything's all right.*

Betyna is all right. She must be. For some time now, she had preferred not to sleep with him. She made her bed on the folding cot in the little room behind the kitchen, intended for the maid. They never had a maid. That little room was supposed to be an office. The computer was supposed to stand there on its own table, and in front of the table, a chair with lumbar support, and on that chair, him, with his programmes on that computer, and his projects in his head. *But who can work in this state, who can buy tables and chairs with lumbar support all the while, in another place in his brain, he must insistently register rustling sounds, and picture continually how they crawl about the branches?* He should have cut down that tree long ago. But those apples: round and full and pecked about by beaks. *Betyna wouldn't understand it, or forgive me. Betyna with her round apples sleeps on the folding cot with one more apple inside her. Ondřej will it be, or Andrea?*

Similar names. Beautiful, almost identical. Oldřich has such a diagram in his head:

> Vowel (*o/a*) + nasal consonant (*n*) + voiced consonant (*d*) + raised alveolar trill (*ř*) / syllabic consonant (*r*) + false diphthong (*ej / ea*) = Ondřej/Andrea.

Technology and linguistics, two old passions of Oldřich's. The pure symbols of the diagram uncluttered with any sort of content creates the perfect scheme for two names for one child. The feminine ending *-ea* with its typical, feminine, falling intonation, the masculine *-ej* with its measured rising intonation. The raised alveolar trill of the ř for the boy expresses that somewhat understandable untidiness typical of a man, whereas the pure *r* of the girl's name bears that unacknowledged hardness of women, which makes them stronger than men.

And so thus must you address twice over one incomprehensible child. They are two approaches to one summit, to the abstract child, of whom all concrete newborns are just imperfect variants, just like all people are merely unsuccessful derivatives of man, of the son of man, the pattern elevated above the poverty of all concrete names, above all vain human destinies.

He had no sooner said it, than the word lightly turned his stomach with its featheriness. *Quickly, away from it! There, where there are no things and no creatures, oh poor me, those dangerous words,* but he had already caught sight of those creatures. He thrust his head beneath his pillow and strove to see *nothing more than the primal foundations of all material things, independent of the light; just some contact points of power, the settings of which constitute a purely geometrical demarcation of reality without those moulded…* searching for the next word, he already knew that it was bad, that this morning, again, he would be flat on his back, impotent. Now, he won't even reach out for his pills, he won't leap into the darkness without preconceptions; he's already conceived those contact points as clearly as the traces of three-toed feet in the mud; already he sees them, evil and ill, the way they hobble and clap their wings, sparse, mousy feathers revealing red scabrous flesh, bare rumps, cloaca, yellow claws, soft coxcombs, feces under feet, the fury in those angry side-set eyes and the worms stuffed in the crop. He sees them always from below, but can't understand how he could have found himself thus beneath them.

Betyna, Ondřej, Andrea, he rasped, and turned to the little bucket ready at the side of his bed. Then he heard the screech of the magpies in the apple tree outside the window. Like they were laughing at him.

"Again, already?" Betyna opened the door to his room. "We're going to have to do something about this. Oldřich, this can't go on."

"Do what?" asked Oldřich, completely abject in his condition, with stomach juices on his chin and chest. *We have to cut down that tree, block up that window!* That's what he wanted to scream, but he swallowed it along with the vomit in his throat.

"I just have to rest a while and not think about it," he whispered hoarsely, instead.

He noticed how all compassion evaporated from Betyna's eyes at the word *rest*. There remained in them but a hard, empty expression, like the furrow between her eyes. She was looking at him with only one eye, *like a bird, o God, like a cormorant* whose beak was about to plunge into the very centre of his sickly heart.

"Betyna, I was just thinking about those names for the child, you know, like we were talking about."

Betyna shrugged her shoulders impatiently. "Yeah, but I've got to go to work. I can't bother with your condition right now. Somebody has to be normal, after all. Especially now."

Oldřich stared dully into his bucket, not knowing whether or not something else was still on the way.

"A normal life, understand? Get yourself washed, get dressed. I'm leaving you the car. Go over to Mr. Kundrát's and take that project he's offering you. It's nothing but a trifle to you, that rudder, or whatever it is they want from you. Take it! It will help you."

"It's not a rudder," Oldřich's shaky cogitations got a firm grip on some project terminology, "it's an aft superstructure with rudder bracket and rudder post."

He pictured to himself the large metal flange in which the rotating peg is set. He saw all of the axes, pivots and dimensions… the whole assembly drawing, black and blue lines in the Blueprint programme. Perspective drawings, side projections and cutaways in CAD-CAM. *These things won't change any realisation. The project will remain perfect, even if they fucked it up at the factory. It is the form of form. But they won't fuck it up. The Odense Lindo Dockyards, with their Lloyds Maritime Registry certificate, won't fuck up the project. They are experienced Northerners, who will build the best ship in the world. A ship with a displacement of fifty thousand registered tonnes brutto with my aft superstructure. A ship as beautiful as Betyna, Betty.*

He looked at her with his bulging eyes and felt his enthusiasm fall like a brittle thing onto a stone floor. *She looks just like a cormorant, ah, one from the North Sea.* The foulness was rising up through his oesophagus. *They are everywhere. Even at the North Pole, and they will fly after you and will caw at you, caw at you from behind your hair until you prefer to jump from the cliff and smash yourself against the rocks or the ice floes just like that brittle thing with all axes splintered and broken.*

"Betyna, you know, I just need to rest, then I will go there. Please, I beg you, give Kundrát a call, call him, let him hang on to it a bit longer, tomorrow, tell him that tomorrow morning I'll come to him and bring my bid."

"Tomorrow morning," she repeated, without a sliver of hope. "Tomorrow morning!" she cried. "This morning I'll be late again because of you. You don't need to rest, you need to get a cure!"

She went off to her belated start of the day while Oldřich wandered about the empty flat in his pyjamas, repeating in a half-whisper a line from an idiotic song: "Prolong the meal a minute more, and there'll be nothing to reach for… Prolong the meal a minute more, and there'll be nothing…" again and again, around and around, so as to block out all other sounds.

"Is it helping you?" Betyna asked.

"It helps," answered Oldřich, knowing that it was impossible.

The situation was murderous; maybe for that reason you could say it was helping. They were sitting in the office of the psychologist, Dr. Nedoma. Oldřich was happy that Betyna had come with him. It was so hard to slip off his pyjamas and dress up in freshly pressed trousers and a shirt, to shave…. he thought that he wouldn't survive it, in his state, as he was constantly yawning and his one desire was to sleep, to lie down. No. He had to go. Betyna was unrelenting. *Nedoma will take us. He knows us. You know how much you'd have to pay anywhere else?* And anyway, if he must, he'll just have to suffer through it. In her nature a responsible Christian faith was mixed with the pragmatism of feet set firmly on the ground. *That sort of firm realist's faith is what settled America, tearing it from the embrace of its quaint pagans.*

He looked at the doctor and at Betyna, as they sat there, ready to help him.

Betyna seemed like a stranger. Oldřich suddenly felt quite all right, and wanted to talk about completely different things. He wanted to ask Bety if they were talking about the same thing when they were pronouncing words about the form of form or the abstract child above all children.

He remembered Betyna's reply: *Well of course, you always have a child, even when you've got a lot of children, it's always singular.* Just like in English, *fish* means not just one fish but all the fish in the net. Or *sheep*, which means one sheep, and all the sheep on the British Isles. *I bet all of those people who work constantly with such plurals, like shepherds or fishermen, constantly use only the singular. Even our fishermen and anglers say 'the fish has too little air; the fish is gathering in the net.' And so I can say that the child is gathering in my uterus.* She said that, and then placed her hand, proprietarily and yet gently, on her stomach, where the pregnancy was not yet showing.

That's how they could talk together, earlier. But the present situation, when the doctor was examining him from the front and Betyna from the side, required a different answer.

"It just kind of started," Oldřich began, encouraged by Dr. Nedoma. "Birds always kind of irritated me, but I always just had a kind of peripheral repugnance for them. If one flew past, a bit too close to me, it kind of turned my stomach. But I didn't dwell on it. I had no idea what ornithophobia might be. Feathered creatures nauseated me, but only to the extent that other people are nauseated by worms, moths and tapeworms — and you don't come across those creatures as often as you do feathered creatures."

It suddenly occurred to him that the word he used for "feathered creatures," *opeřenci,* was dangerously similar to *opera.*

"And how did it develop, over time?" Nedoma asked.

"At the start, it was kind of a game. I didn't take it seriously for a long time. It just somehow happened that I began to consider them my enemies. I began to play hide and seek with them. I convinced myself that they were always watching me, persecuting me. They are everywhere, anyway. Have you ever noticed that, doctor, that they are everywhere? You can even meet them in the cellar, those small ones, brown and grey as mice, and in caves… I read about it."

"In caves you'll find bats, rather, and I for one admit that those are rather frightful."

"I've got nothing against bats. They don't bother me. The bat is a mammal. He has fur, whereas birds, they are completely different creatures. I think that they must hate us, if only for the reason that we don't have beaks and wings and… sorry…"

Oldřich took a few deep breaths and assured himself with a glance that, nearby, a bucket had been readied, along with paper towels. Betyna thought of everything.

"At first, I thought that I'd just made it all up. But then I realised that that's the way it is. Each time I met them, I became more convinced of it. Have you ever looked a bird in the eye?"

"Probably not," the doctor replied, amused.

"Well, I don't advise it. Such hatred. Basically, the bird is only longing for you to die so that he might feast on your corpse. And that thought about death, it begins to grow in you, just like a cuckoo chick; soon it stifles all other thoughts, so that you don't have anything else in your mind. All you do is imagine some sort of horrid titmouse or shrike sitting on your body and pecking out your eyes."

Oldřich covered his eyes and went on, hidden in his own private darkness:

"Doctor, I didn't come here because birds are awful. I know, I also know, that snakes are horrid, as well as, I don't know, bacteria even. I came here, or rather, Betyna brought me here, because I can't help but keep thinking about this, just like a person has to keep thinking about a sore thumb or some sort of unpaid social insurance. You know what I'm talking about: whole nights of anxiety, sweaty feet — unbearable. The horrid exhaustion. You know what I'm talking about?"

"You got me spot on with those unpaid bills," the doctor laughed.

Oldřich glanced at Betyna, who sat with her elbows on her knees, her chin on her fists and her eyes wide open in surprise.

"But now that we're having a chat about this together," the doctor continued, "don't you feel a little better now that you've expressed yourself in front of other people?"

"No," Oldřich replied, measuring with his eyes the distance to the bucket. "With me it's like," he began, giving off a bitter laugh, "that even when I think about my own bird, you know, my penis..."

"Of course," the doctor nodded, and Betyna turned away.

"...it disgusts me, merely on account of that metaphor."

"Now, that's interesting. That's a difficult verbalisation. You're having difficulties with that? I think that we can speak about everything here, openly, right?" the doctor continued, directing a careful apology towards Betyna.

"I am."

"But if you used a different metaphor?"

"You can't just switch things like that."

"You're right about that. You'd really need to practise something like that," the doctor stated.

Oldřich glanced at Betyna's back, her sloping shoulders, and sensed the disgust she felt. *Can't take this one back,* he said to himself, *as if you could take anything back ever. You never step twice into the same woman… river, that is*, he corrected himself, and strove to continue his conversation with the doctor.

"Well, try to tell me what exactly it is that disgusts you about birds. Their talons? Their beaks?" the doctor encouraged.

"That too," Oldřich assumed, imagining in his mind their hollow bones, strong sternum, air sacs, muscle contractions, cloaca, crop. His constructor's mind told him that all this constituted a perfectly dynamic structure, nothing repulsive.

"Mostly their difference from us, and their fury," he said aloud. "Birds are merciless."

"Have you ever experienced a traumatic encounter with birds? Were you ever attacked, as a child, by a rooster or a goose? Swans can be aggressive, too."

"Yeah, perhaps. Maybe some bird did injure me. Must have. But I don't remember it. If so, I'd have had this aversion from always."

"Aversion? From always? No. Nobody ever has an aversion to something from always. Newborn children have no aversions. Those come only with experience."

"But I can't remember any sort of experience like that."

"Of course you can't. You'd conquer it, if you could. We'd have to put you under hypnosis."

"Put me under…" Oldřich suddenly felt ill at the thought of what he'd have to remember under hypnosis. He lunged at the ready bucket and threw up into it forcefully, as if it were expected of him that he would fill it full. The worst thing about it was the consciousness that even then there'd be something left behind. The expectation of further nauseas hence unto the end of the world twisted in him like a revolting rag he'd never be able to fully puke out. *If that rag happens to be my immortal soul, well, thank you very much.*

He collapsed to the floor and lay there, breathing heavily. Nedoma and Betyna stood at the window, their backs turned to the room, in a strangely understanding discretion.

"I'm ready now," Oldřich said, after having wiped himself clean with the paper towels. "Where can I spill this out?"

"The toilet is in the bathroom," Nedoma said gently, showing him the door.

After the interruption, when they were all sitting at their places again, Nedoma continued: "Permit me to ask you one more, last question, before we move on to speak about therapy. Tell me when it was that you first experienced a real attack of ornithophobia. But a real one now, one that you couldn't defend against. I'm not talking about any sort of minor discomfort — all of us experience that. Tell me: when was the first time that it was stronger than you?"

"Doctor, I really wouldn't be able to tell you."

"That's why you must."

"I don't know. Betyna?" Oldřich turned to his wife in deep despair. In her eyes, for the first time, he read genuine fear. She was afraid that he'd say what she thought he'd say.

"You've got to say it," she told him, in a near whisper.

"OK then. The first time that I had an attack that was simply unbearable, was when Betyna told me that we were expecting a child."

He knew well what he was doing when he said that, and for that reason, Betyna's expression didn't really surprise him. Nor was he surprised by her resentment when they got back into the car. He felt that, if they'd had two cars, she'd have taken the other. When the back of his hand grazed her thigh at his shifting into fifth gear, she angrily tossed that leg over the other and sat as far away from him as her seatbelt allowed her to.

"They don't have a rooster any more," Míla Kučera, his old classmate from the rural elementary school, told Oldřich.

"So, no rooster? That's stupid," said Oldřich, disappointed. "I already wanted to get that over with."

"They have turkeys, but they're big ones," said Míla.

"Rooster or turkey, it's all the same. A turkey's a kind of rooster, isn't he? A dick's a dick."[36]

----

36   In Czech, rooster = *kohout*, penis = *kokot*.

"Why is it you want so to learn how to kill? I don't know what you need it for. You always buy your poultry frozen, don't you?"

"Listen, can you do this for me, or not?" Oldřich insisted.

"Sure. I promised you, and I'll keep my promise. But only if there's nothing stupid behind it all."

"There is, but it's a necessary stupidity."

"Well, it's your money."

"It's my money," Oldřich brought the matter to a close, as the delivery van turned into the poultry farm.

They got out of the van in front of a long, low structure, from which the gobbling voices of many turkeys could be heard. Míla went inside to get everything ready, while Oldřich fought through many minutes of anguish. Then Míla returned and led him into the place in which the therapy was to be carried out.

"You've got to go now!" he said.

After about a half hour, Oldřich opened the door and let Míla back inside.

The head remained on the block; the body was lain inside a large tin crate. The utensils and the rag were in a container filled with water.

"Well, this has been a day! I was already telling myself that if you don't kill him, he'll kill you," rang the voice of Míla.

"It was no clear thing at the start," Oldřich explained, undoing the bloody rubber apron. "My heart is still beating like a hammer."

"Well, he was a big one. It's not like wringing the neck of a dove," Míla stated, casting a learned eye on the butchered animal. "You did a good job. Beautiful, in fact, for a city boy. Clean. Direct, just like I told you."

"The hardest thing was to take him in hand. After that, it just went on by itself almost," Oldřich explained.

"Same with everything. Until you do it yourself, you don't know what it's all about," Míla said, philosophically.

"And that's why you're afraid of it," Oldřich finished the thought.

"What? You're not being serious? You were afraid of roosters and turkeys?"

"No, of killing."

"Well, I get that. A person has to work up the guts, if I can put it like that."

"So then, I'm off," said Oldřich. Suddenly, he didn't want to stand around chatting any more.

"Wait a bit. You can't take him just like that! Your good woman would give you a nice blessing for that! Let me have it prepared for you."

"You know what? I don't even want him."

"Are you crazy? You paid for him."

"But I don't want him."

"No, it can't be like that," Míla said resolutely. "That wasn't the deal. So I won't prepare it. But I'm not going to throw it out. That's meat, and you don't throw food into the garbage."

"All right then, prepare it," Oldřich said, with a resigned wave of the hand. "That's part of it, I guess."

"You know that it's all part of it. Don't be soft."

But he wasn't soft. Not as he drove through the evening landscape with the dead bird in his trunk, nor when he was sitting with Betyna on the bench beneath the apple tree, the bench covered with birdshit, considering once more the names for their child, who for the first time was nearing them from afar.

The aft superstructure with rudder bracket and rudder post of the transatlantic ship was assuming clear contours on his computer, thanks to his precise calculations. Everything was in order, as much as anything can be. Only from time to time did his heart pain him on behalf of that heart, which had been beating so close to his own heart, and before it ceased beating.[37]

---

37   The Czech original ends with an untranslatable pun. The final sentence reads (*Obě -i- po -b- v předchozí větě mohou být nahrazena ypsilon a význam se nezmění),* meaning "Both of the 'i's after the 'b's in the last sentence may be replaced by 'y's without changing the meaning." This has to do with the Czech homonyms *bít* ("beat") and *být* ("be"). Thus, the sentence that speaks of a "heart, which had been beating so close to his own heart, and then ceased beating," can be changed to a grammatically perfect, and appropriate sentence reading "the heart, which had been so close to his own heart, and then ceased to be," merely by the substitution of the vowels in the two verbs.

GIRL TERRORIST

"Can an innocent picture exist? What sort of question is that? Innocent, how?" Hans cast his eyes around at all the pictures.

"A picture simply and undeceivingly relating to reality, without irony or exaggeration or any other broken viewpoints," Michal, the painter, developed his thought.

"By that do you mean, a painting that existed obviously, if someone really cared for it, if it was socially possible and profitable? I don't know. Otherwise, certainly it exists; only no lights are trained upon it."

"So you think that real innocence exists?"

"I don't know. But it ought to, at least for women's sake."

"What do you mean?"

"Just that!"

It was hard for Hans to talk about this, because he had been carrying a woman inside him all his life long. Even though he was indubitably a husband and a father of his children, he felt femininity at the basis of all his sentiments.

Ever since he was a little boy, in that blessed age before the first awakenings of emotion by which the pubescent child, violently thrown into the world of sex, is knocked off balance, he looked at the world rather through the eyes of his mother, than those of his father. He thought it would remain that way. It couldn't. It was a vain thought, just like his desire to find his own place in the world that he would not have to leave again, where he could put down roots. For that reason he wept over each mile-stone or boundary stone which he had to pass by. He suffered each time his parents re-arranged the furniture in the flat, yearning all the time for the former constellations as if for a lost home. As a grown man he had trouble leaving places behind, even hotel rooms. He figured that this unease had begun to sprout in him exactly then, when, tossing off for the first time, he wounded the until then peacefully present, graceful woman inside him.

He wasn't a homosexual, neither a latent one, nor one of any other stripe. Nor was he ever attracted to cross-dressing. On the contrary. When he saw female attributes adorning some man, he was disgusted. Drag queens made him want to throw up — those little prissies with their stuffed bras and painted lips offended the woman, the existence of whom no one knew: the woman, who was also Hans. Pornographic magazines likewise made him ill. He grew sick at himself looking at those magazines, sick at the treason he committed by his hungry glomming of women spreading their legs in front of the camera, and thus in front of the whole world. When he bought a magazine like that, and used it, and threw it away in the ashcan, he understood what sin meant. *Not a sin against God, that is, against the father, for the father would perhaps understand even such actions. No, that was a sin against her, against that primal being, who lives lost in some sort of labyrinth, in an unseen, but felt system of underground caves, there, where our primal people live, with whom we are connected by a bond as thin as Ariadne's thread…*

"A thread which obviously can't be broken, but later…" Hans suddenly started in fear, because he wasn't sure when exactly he had begun to think aloud.

"Later? What, later? Go on," Michal encouraged him.

"Later? Later we can paint any sort of cunt on the wall and pretend that we've found the entrance into the cave of creation."

"I wouldn't dramatise it so," Michal responded with a nasty casualness. "On the contrary, I believe that every cunt on every wall and every porno girl can all the same point the way to those primal beings, of whom you speak. The loss of innocence is a fact; the fallen world is fallen. You are nothing more than a romantic on steroids, but even so you're not consistent. If you were a consistent, real poet, you'd write a great poem and die young. You don't survive the broken thread! But you bumble around for forty years, as you say, in the labyrinth. You make love to women, you father children, you establish households just like we all do, and moreover you consider it all to be wrong. In the best case, Hans, this is infantile narcissism. In the worst, its simple hypocrisy, snobbery."

"I thought you were a painter," Hans responded angrily. "But you're also a psychologist. All you need is a pipe to be cleaning while I spill out my guts to you. I know, you probably don't have any problems with pornography. It inspires your work. It's all the rage today, anyway. Why do all you painters grub around in smut?"

"I don't know what other painters grub around in, but I do have a problem with pornography — that's why I exploit it. It seems insincere to me. I'm even ashamed of those magazines. I only buy those that are sealed in plastic — I don't trust the traffickers and all the other ones about. Who knows what they do there? I'm obsessed with the thought that I might catch some sort of disease. Well, that goes with it all, that danger, just like the strange, phoney normality of all those practices. I paint those absurd situations and positions in order to bring it out of me, drag it out into the light, so that I might quite calmly inspect that whole bizarre circus."

"The bizarre is what threatens the world," Hans said, with fury, "everything today must be somehow dislocated from its natural joints and shouted about and put up for display like a shop window. Let me tell you something. You people don't paint pictures any more. You paint adverts for painting and all of you are going to end up in advertising anyway, and then you'll be hiding on the crapper some day, leafing through Munch for example and whispering *Oh man, that's how you do it!*"

"Of course. And none of that touches you, because you wander about babbling in a noble delirium about primal beings."

Hans said nothing in response. The picture of a thin girl sitting on a blood-red sofa flickered through his head. She was looking him straight in the eye and lifted him beyond that conversation to a sphere of pure pain, and in the face of her, Hans and his friend the painter were as helpless as little children.

When the story of the Chechen commando's terrorist attack at the Moscow theatre became known, something moved in Hans again. It was as if he were just continuing an interrupted conversation. Fear began to spread. The theatre community found itself faced with the tommy guns of despairingly determined fighters with nothing to lose, threatening innocent women and children and men with death, because their own innocent women and children and men had been already bombed to smithereens in Grozny. The heavy armoured mechanisms of the Russian state took their positions around the theatre. It was clear to everyone that there were not going to be any negotiations. There's only going to be killing. Inside the Bolshoi Theatre was the mixed group of the terrified and despairingly determined; outside were the innumerable divisions of the armed forces, waiting on their orders, and in the outermost circle, bewildered people, who had no influence on anything that was happening.

In the auditorium, mixed in among the hostages, sit Chechen women, the wives of fighters who had been killed. On their bodies are suicide vests, in their hands, detonators. It is they who are to become deadly weapons in case their unmeetable demands should not be met.

Hans and Michal and other people having no influence on the events transpiring, vainly sought in torturous conversations at least the trace of a just solution to this bizarre situation, in which everything had been knocked out of joint.

Then came the attack. The special forces broke through the ceilings and floors and pumped in a gas that killed the greater portion of the people inside. Then the soldiers in gas masks delivered the coup de grâce in person to all the terrorists, male and female, and from then on it was just the general Russian routine: people choking and dying in crowded ambulances, while the army chemists refused to reveal the makeup of the weaponised gas to the doctors; family members searching in vain for those who haven't contacted them… A pyrrhic victory.

"At least the jackets didn't explode."

"The women terrorists were probably paralysed before they could detonate them."

"So why did they go in there and shoot them in the head?"

"To make sure, I guess."

"But that's idiotic. The gas took only a few seconds to finish them off. People pulled their clothes over their heads, crawled under the chairs…. How many seconds do you need to press a button?"

"You think that, in the end, they had pity on their hostages?"

"Only God knows how it was, but I think that the next ones won't wait to detonate."

A few weeks after the attack Michal invited Hans to his atelier, and again they talked over the idea of the innocent picture.

"This one might interest you," Michal said, turning around a picture that had been resting against the wall.

It showed a woman's head emerging from under a grey plastic tarp. A pool of blood expanded from her dark hair.

"The dead girl terrorist. I painted it after a photo in the news," Michal said matter-of-factly.

Hans bent down close to the very canvas, as if the better to make out her features.

"Who exactly does she look like?" said Hans, as if he were posing the question to himself.

"Well, you," Michal interjected, embarrassingly.

"Me?"

"At least I wanted her to look like you."

"It worked. You got it," Hans coughed out, and then grew quiet. "Will you sell me that painting?"

"Well, I thought you'd want it, but you can't have it. It's already sold, and at a very good price."

"Who bought it?"

"Some moneybags. Owner of some clubs. He's paid for it already, and is about to take it away, but I wanted you to see it first. So I'll deliver it to him tomorrow."

"But why this one, exactly? You've got a lot of pictures that would better suit clubs."

"He only wanted this one. He said that it would be wacky to have a picture like that in a tavern. It would make a strong impression."

"So we'll go and look at it there, even though I detest clubs," Hans said somewhat nostalgically, gazing into the dead eyes, which lifted him into a sphere of pure pain.

RAY BRADBURY

"The fact that a doctor diagnoses his own illness won't cure him. Like a condemned man in his cell, he only knows how he will die. But anyway, it's good to see the path before one, each single step, up to that last one leading into the unknown. To know what one can still do, especially when a deadline has been established. Here, doctors have no protection; here doctors become patients." The old man looked up at the sun and spoke and spoke, as if his words would protect him from something.

"Ah, those words — *patients* and *protection*. Words burdened with the weight of time. Our time, these five and seventy years which we've been given on the arc of time, somewhere after the incarnation of Christ. It seems to me that the very distortion of these words is a direct result of our work, our building of a new world. And there are other sins on our account. The reversed flow of rivers, dried lakes, harbours in the desert. But that is all far, far from here, where the patients are, since there are only patients now — that is our fate, the reality of our days."

The old doctor, Karel Chudoba, was making the best of the morning, on a verandah chair at the summer house. After the death of his wife Sofie and a vain, yearlong attempt to live alone, he finally did what he had always refused to do — he entrusted himself to the care of his children. The diagnosis, which he presented himself with, and which was confirmed by his younger colleagues, demanded intensive care. Because no one has yet measured the steps of progressive Alzheimer's disease.

Each morning he had some clear hours. They were like a kind of floating island, which he never knew when it would appear, and when it would sink again into the strange, monotone brilliance. As long as he was still able to recall his state or its progression and compare it to something, it seemed like the glowing white projection screen when the film running through the spools suddenly snaps. This was the periphery of his reality, and even Plato couldn't surmise what happens then, in that timeless region, from which he emerged only at the next appearance of the island. He somehow didn't suffer on its account, he just again became aware of the fact that, when his consciousness returned, it was morning. A beautiful time of day, which must be exploited to the full, thinking a few thoughts through to the end. It was just like a lace-maker, going blind, who pulls tight the last eyelets of the pattern, which she already can't see, from memory.

"Those words once possessed their own beautiful, inviolate meanings."

Plato believed that he was still speaking to his son, or to his grandson Timoteus, but it is just as likely that he was already left alone on his veranda with the morning sun; that the young man had already gone off to his own business. He simply kept speaking, because he believed that words have a sense, even if there is no one to hear them.

"In Latin, *patient*, besides its meaning of 'he who suffers,' also had that other meaning of patience. A patient, meaning he who accepts his suffering as a task, as the next chapter in his life. He is patient and quiet, so as not to miss hope passing by, or liberation, even if that liberation is death. But we have made our patients into impatient, hysterical beggars, who shield their eyes before their task. They're not waiting for help; they chase help away with their fevered demands of health, of freedom from suffering, freedom from death. Our promising the impossible has taught them to beg, to bribe, to seek protection.

"And protection…"

Chudoba smiled, calmed at the thought that he had arrived at the second term that he wished to explain to the young man quite logically.

"In the past, protection has been the defence of the weak by the stronger. It has been our mother's embrace, our father's arm, the ruler's guarantee, the Laws of God, by which one could live and in which he could safely die. That was protection. We've made a business of it, a comfort that can be bought, an illusion pumped into our veins, a lie. You understand, boy — that's how the world has changed because of your parents' actions. That's how I see it, as long as I can see anything. Are you still here?"

"Yes, Grandpa," answered the eighteen-year-old boy, leaning against the railing and impatiently looking out into the landscape. He had to keep an eye on Gramps (he wouldn't use that word in front of his mother or his father; as a child he detested it. But now he accepted it from the lips of a girl, who had grown up in different circumstances. When he had excused himself, *that he couldn't come tonight, because his parents had entrusted him with the care of a sick person…* she brought his long winded explanation to an end shortly with: *OK, you've got to keep an eye on Gramps. I understand*, and they put off their date until another time). At first, he wanted to listen to music. But then he left his earbuds in his pocket. After all, this might be the last time he gets to listen to Grampa, before the old man loses consciousness completely.

"Yeah, Grampa. I'm here."

"That's good. If you weren't, I'd have to invent you. I know that I'm impossible. I have Alzheimer's, and everything is falling away from me. Until literally everything will be lost, and there will remain nothing more than my poorly functioning body. Saliva will start to drip from my open mouth; I'll crumble and slobber my food over my clothes like a little child. I know. I've had patients like that. I know exactly what's waiting for me. But what I don't know, my boy, or have already forgotten, is whether you're my son, or my grandson…"

"Your grandson. Timik."

"Yes, Timik, Timoteus. Timik, I don't know what's waiting for you, and now I'll never find out. Those birds are flying really high. I can't tell if they're crows or gulls. I don't already know if it's spring or fall. The sun is like it appears in the spring, and like it appears in the fall, in spring…"

"It's fall," said Timoteus, but the old man couldn't hear him already. In his head he heard only the flap-flapping of the film after the last frames had run through the sprockets of the wheel near the lens, leaving nothing more on the screen but white undifferentiated light. While Tim was helping him back into the room and laying him down on the bed, he behaved like an obedient robot.

"I put him to bed," Tim said to his mother, when he came down to the ground floor of the summer house.

"You're a good boy," the woman answered him. She was pretty; she had preserved her attractive looks into late middle age. Only a few wrinkles around the eyes and mouth and a stray grey hair here and there hinted at the fact that this girl had actually passed over the hill and was now on the downward part of the path.

I have no regrets, Emilie, whom everyone called Ema, always said to herself whenever the conversation turned to aging. For just beyond that crest of the hill, which, looking back, she reached somewhere between her thirty-eighth and thirty-ninth year, there opened up such vistas as, when she was a girl, she could never have even imagined.

"You know, Grandpa's not asleep. He's just not conscious, not here."

"I know, but that's so peculiar. When exactly is his consciousness here? Or does he stop existing, and then jump to life again, like some sort of generator when it's flipped on?"

"I imagine it's like this. Grandpa suddenly goes away from his current home for a bit. That damaged brain of his, I suppose, is no longer able to keep contact with it, or at most only for a couple of hours every day, like some sort of half-charged transmitter. The soul isn't completely enmeshed with the body, as a person might wish. I know something about that, Timoty," she said, and looked at her son the way she had back then, when she had opened her eyes again upon a world she had no longer expected to see.

You know something about that, the boy said in his soul, his gaze falling upon his mother's left wrist. She wore a few silver bracelets there. Not that they could cover anything, really, but they could draw the onlooker's attention away from the white scars that inconspicuously signified the moment when Emilie Ema vaulted over the hill crest. In Timi's memory, those scars were still as red as fresh cracks, like the realisation of how supposedly safe childhood is from the shedding of blood. Just now it began to be clear to him that that little death provided his mother with an end to horrifying scenes, screams in the night and dashing off, searching for pills in her handbag and searching for solace in the arms of others, searching for tenderness on the ruins of self-mutilation. He had never been completely able to stifle the memory of his discovery in the bathtub that day, but he lived, as if he had been. He steeled himself to the reappearance of his father, who entered their flat for the first time after two years, led by a doctor and two nurses. Tim chiefly wished to leave himself that: that his father remained with them, even when his mother returned from the hospital, and remained so obviously, as if it had never been otherwise. It was chiefly with that that Tim wished to scar closed the traces of his mother's wounds.

He wanted to remember and he did remember how his father bought the summer house, in which he was now living with his mother and grandfather, all the while he, the wealthy man that Tim honoured, although he could never really draw close to him, worked in town and came here only on the weekends. He always asked Tim to accompany him to church on Sunday, and he never refused.

Mama (the word is liberating to him, yet he cannot allow it to pass through his lips just yet, or, if ever in the hearing of another person, then only in the presence of that girl, before whom he is most ashamed to pronounce it), Mama also works, but here in the summer house. She translates books that arrive by the invisible roads of the internet and become incarnate on the paper pages sliding out of the laser printer, which is quiet and solid and does not emit any hysterical sounds. Then the books take over his mother's table and come alive with piles of symbols, incomprehensible glosses and notes on the margins of the pages, until again they disappear, sent forth to invisible publishers by e-mail.

"Why did you name me Timoty? I've been wanting to ask you that for a long time."

"And I've been waiting for you to ask. It's a name from a book. That book gave you your name."

"You call the Bible 'a book'?"

"No, I wouldn't allow myself to," smiled Emilie Ema. "Of course, Timoteus is a Biblical name. You know the Epistles to Timothy. But Timoty is a name from the *Martian Chronicles* of Raymond Bradbury."

"I haven't read it."

"That's too bad. It's a good book. You can, we have it on the shelves here," she said and at the same time was pained at the thought that after that recommendation Tim would probably have a hard time reading it. He's like her: he doesn't gladly accept what he hasn't discovered himself.

"In the last story of the book, I think, which is called 'The Million Year Picnic,' there is a boy named Timoty. His parents escape to Mars just before the outbreak of the atomic war, in which the entire Earth is destroyed."

"So it's a kind of science fiction?"

"Not just a kind of science fiction, it's good science fiction. We discovered Bradbury in the late sixties of the last century. The

Third World War seemed just about to begin. A few years before that, Khrushchev had tried to place nuclear weapons on Cuba. And then there was the moon landing."

"We learned about that in school."

"But perhaps they didn't teach you in school that the atmosphere of those days, when we were waiting — Who's going to push the button first and send off the first ICBM? — They called it the politics of deterrence — *odstrašení,* in Czech, the politics of fear. There is a beautiful English word, *overkill.* How would you translate it?"

"Kill — *zabít*; overkill — *přezabít,* I suppose, more than kill: kill through and through," tried Tim. "Yes, that's really, really strong."

"Yes, and it's a fitting term. The world was a little crazy back then, and we were all young."

Emilie Ema lit up a cigarette, something she did only rarely. She offered the packet to her son, who never smoked at all.

"No, it makes me ill," Tim declined, embarrassed.

"You're wise," his mother nodded. "We weren't at all smart back then. When I think back on those times," Emilie said, dreamily drawing her eyelids closed, "It's as if I heard Jimi Hendrix's guitar…"

"I know Hendrix. He's good. A classic. I would never have reckoned you for a Hendrix fan."

"Well, these days all we listen to is classical music. But back then… it's as if I could hear that guitar again, and the police sirens and the news about outer space and the demonstrations, the horrors of the Vietnam War, My Lai, new films about drugs and free love, and in the end, in the end of course the Russian tanks. I was still a young girl when I saw the long columns of tanks cutting through the canola fields of Polabí.[38] A few years later there remained only the jammed transmissions of Voice of America, each night at nine o'clock. Those jammers screeched and crackled wildly, but quite differently from Hendrix. You were born a long time after that. Your name links your father's Evangelical tradition with our — it might sound odd to you, but I'll say it nonetheless — dream of escaping from this world."

---

38   Lowlands north of Prague.

When on the next morning old Dr. Chudoba's island of consciousness miraculously emerged from the sea again, Emilie sent Tim to take him on a walk in the garden. They walked about together, slowly, among the fruit trees and the vegetable plots, on which the greens, bent beneath the first autumn frosts, were living out their last. He wasn't thinking about patients or protection any more. He felt a kind of anxiety within himself, an urgent communication of a sort, which he needed to give his son — whom by mistake he took Tim to be. They were quite similar after all, father and son; the only thing that differentiated them, perhaps, was time — and Karel Chudoba had nothing more to do with time.

"You know, my boy, a person has to return to where he belongs. Home. Even if that home isn't a welcoming one. And even if you had to return only to accept punishment, you've got to return. That punishment is a part of your life, too."

"But we are home," Tim replied.

"No, we don't belong here. We have to return home. Even before they send us there in a sealed casket or a plastic bag, boy."

"Where? Send us where?"

"As if you didn't know!" the old man said, testily. "Along there, there along the road, then the alleyway to the train station and then the train. It's not far from here. Just a couple of stations. I can't remember just now what it's called — this little town in Galicia. They have train stations there, and the platforms are set with wooden tiles. I lived there a few years, and now I can't remember the name. It's this head of mine, you know, I'm suffering from Alzheimer's. Pretty soon I won't know a single thing — this I know for sure."

He smiled at Tim strangely. His smile shot through Tim like something monstrous, threatening, as if joy had turned itself inside out.

"But, Grandpa…"

"It's a kind of paradox, son," Chudoba calmed his supposed son with a quick gesture of his hand. "I can quite clearly see the edges of my blindness. I know for sure that I will cease to know. But that's all right — it can happen to anyone. God allows it. But do you know what God does not forgive?"

Again that smile of false teeth between skewed lips.

"God does not forgive those who escape. And I must stop escaping; I must go there."

They had arrived at the garden gate. Karel Chudoba took the latch in hand and led Tim underneath the cosy shade of the apple tree.

"Grandpa, I think that we should go back," Tim said, halting his grandfather.

"Yes, you're right," the old man nodded, and gripped his son's hand tightly in his own. They exited the shade together into the burning light of the September day.

ACKNOWLEDGEMENTS

This translation is based on the Czech original of *Možná, že odcházíme*, collected in Volume I of the *Sebrané díla* of Jan Balabán (*Povídky*), edited by Petr Hruška and published by Host of Brno in 2010. It is identical with the original printings of 2004 and 2007, also published by Host.

The publication of this translation was made possible through the generosity of a grant from the Czech Translation Programme of the Ministry of Culture of the Czech Republic. I wish to express my sincere gratitude for this aid.

I also wish to thank all the folk at Glagoslav for their expertise and help, and for affording me the opportunity to bring this beautiful book to the attention of the English reading public.

ABOUT THE AUTHOR

Jan Balabán was born in Šumperk, a town near the city of Olomouc in what was at the time Czechoslovakia, on 29 January 1961. He was raised in the city of Ostrava, which lies some 92 kilometres southwest of his birthplace. It is this city that forms the backdrop for most of his fiction.

He entered the University of Olomouc in the 1980s, where he studied Czech and English. Upon graduation, he began work as a technical translator in Ostrava. Up until the Velvet Revolution and the fall of Communism in 1989, his works were clandestinely published; like his brother the painter Daniel Balabán and so many other artists of his generation, he was a dissident.

Before his sudden and untimely death on 23 April 2010, he had published several books, mostly collections of short stories, in the now unfettered press of the free Czech Republic. These are: *Středověk* (Middle Age, 1995) *Boží lano* (The Rope of God, 1998), *Prázdniny* (Holidays, 1998), *Možná, že odcházíme* (Maybe We're Leaving, 2004), and *Jsme tady* (Here We Are, 2006). He also published two novels, Černý beran (The Black Ram, 2000) and *Kudy šel anděl* (Which Way the Angel Went, 2003), a screenplay *Srdce draka* (The Heart of a Dragon, 2001) and a stageplay entitled *Bezruč?!* (No Hands?!, 2009) in collaboration with Ivan Motýl. *Zeptej se táty* (Ask Dad), the manuscript of a novel that he was working on at his death, was posthumously published in 2010.

ABOUT THE TRANSLATOR

Charles S. Kraszewski (b. 1962) is a poet and translator, writing in both English and Polish. He is the author of three volumes of original verse: *Beast* (2013), *Diet of Nails* (2014) and *Chanameed* (2014). Among his translations from the Polish published by Glagoslav are Adam Mickiewicz's *Forefathers' Eve* (2016) and Stanisław Wyspiański's *Acropolis: the Wawel Plays* (2017). His translation of Czech author Jaroslav Hašek's *Secret History of My Sojourn in Russia* was published by Glagoslav in 2017. He is a member of the Union of Polish Writers Abroad (London) and of the Association of Polish Writers (Kraków).

TIME OF THE OCTOPUS

by Anatoly Kucherena

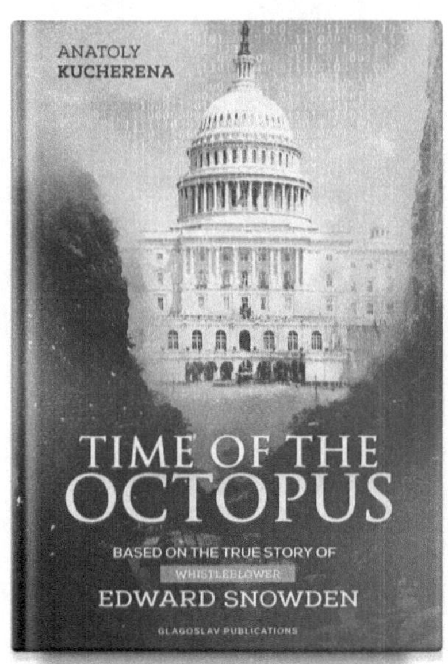

A frightening, prophetic vision of our world...
In Moscow's Sheremetyevo airport, fugitive US intelligence officer
Joshua Kold is held in limbo, unable to leave the airport's transit area.
He is on the run, after blowing the lid off the terrifying reach of covert
American global surveillance operations. Will the Russian authorities
grant him asylum, or will they hand him over the clutches of the
global octopus eager for revenge for his betrayal?
As this gripping psychological and political thriller unfolds, a Moscow
lawyer takes Kold to a secret bunker and grills him intently on just why
he did it. Upon Kold's answers hang not only his own fate, but much,
much more as the true extent of this chilling 1984 world unfolds.
Anatoly Kucherena is the famous Russian lawyer who took on the case
of the American whistleblower Edward Snowden whose revelations
about US intelligence operations sent shockwaves around the world in
2013. Time of the Octopus is a fiction, but it is based on Kucherena's
own interviews with Snowden at Sheremetyevo, and provides the
basis for Oliver Stone's major Hollywood movie 'Snowden' starring
Joseph Gordon-Levitt, one of the movie events of 2016...

Buy it > www.glagoslav.com

Tsunami

by Anatoly Kurchatkin

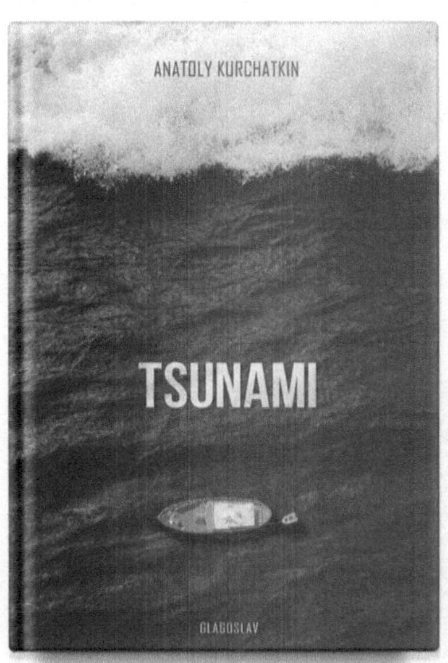

Anatoly Kurchatkin's novel, set in Russia and Thailand, ranges in time from the Brezhnev years of political stagnation, when Soviet values seemed set to endure for eternity, through Gorbachev's Perestroika and the following tumultuous and disorientating decades. Under the surface, ancient currents are influencing the destinies of mathematician Rad, art gallery owner Jenny, entrepreneur (and spy?) Dron, American investor Chris, redundant Soviet diplomat Yelena and Thai playboy Tony in a rapidly globalizing world of laptop computers, mobile phones, credit cards and international finance. The fourteenth-century battle in which the Prince of Muscovy, inspired by St Sergius of Radonezh, defeated the Golden Horde of the Mongol Empire foreshadows a modern struggle for the soul of Russia.

Tsunami was shortlisted for the Russian Booker Prize and the
Russo-Italian Moscow-Penne Prize.

Buy it > www.glagoslav.com

A Brown Man in Russia
Lessons Learned on the Trans-Siberian
by Vijay Menon

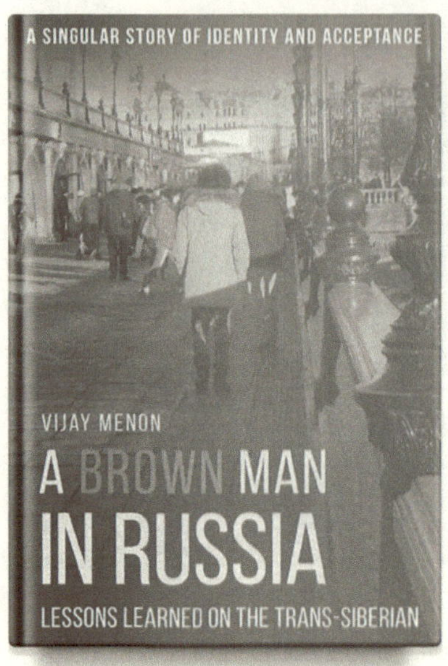

A Brown Man in Russia describes the fantastical travels of a young, colored American traveler as he backpacks across Russia in the middle of winter via the Trans-Siberian. The book is a hybrid between the curmudgeonly travelogues of Paul Theroux and the philosophical works of Robert Pirsig. Styled in the vein of Hofstadter, the author lays out a series of absurd, but true stories followed by a deeper rumination on what they mean and why they matter. Each chapter presents a vivid anecdote from the perspective of the fumbling traveler and concludes with a deeper lesson to be gleaned. For those who recognize the discordant nature of our world in a time ripe for demagoguery and for those who want to make it better, the book is an all too welcome antidote. It explores the current global climate of despair over differences and outputs a very different message – one of hope and shared understanding. At times surreal, at times inappropriate, at times hilarious, and at times deeply human, *A Brown Man in Russia* is a reminder to those who feel marginalized, hopeless, or endlessly divided that harmony is achievable even in the most unlikely of places.

Buy it > www.glagoslav.com

Glagoslav Publications Catalogue

- *The Time of Women* by Elena Chizhova
- *Andrei Tarkovsky: The Collector of Dreams*
  by Layla Alexander-Garrett
- *Andrei Tarkovsky - A Life on the Cross* by Lyudmila Boyadzhieva
- *Sin* by Zakhar Prilepin
- *Hardly Ever Otherwise* by Maria Matios
- *Khatyn* by Ales Adamovich
- *The Lost Button* by Irene Rozdobudko
- *Christened with Crosses* by Eduard Kochergin
- *The Vital Needs of the Dead* by Igor Sakhnovsky
- *The Sarabande of Sara's Band* by Larysa Denysenko
- *A Poet and Bin Laden* by Hamid Ismailov
- *Watching The Russians (Dutch Edition)* by Maria Konyukova
- *Kobzar* by Taras Shevchenko
- *The Stone Bridge* by Alexander Terekhov
- *Moryak* by Lee Mandel
- *King Stakh's Wild Hunt* by Uladzimir Karatkevich
- *The Hawks of Peace* by Dmitry Rogozin
- *Harlequin's Costume* by Leonid Yuzefovich
- *Depeche Mode* by Serhii Zhadan
- *The Grand Slam and other stories (Dutch Edition)*
  by Leonid Andreev
- *METRO 2033 (Dutch Edition)* by Dmitry Glukhovsky
- *METRO 2034 (Dutch Edition)* by Dmitry Glukhovsky
- *A Russian Story* by Eugenia Kononenko
- *Herstories, An Anthology of New Ukrainian Women Prose Writers*
- *The Battle of the Sexes Russian Style* by Nadezhda Ptushkina
- *A Book Without Photographs* by Sergey Shargunov
- *Down Among The Fishes* by Natalka Babina
- *disUNITY* by Anatoly Kudryavitsky
- *Sankya* by Zakhar Prilepin
- *Wolf Messing* by Tatiana Lungin
- *Good Stalin* by Victor Erofeyev

- *Solar Plexus* by Rustam Ibragimbekov
- *Don't Call me a Victim!* by Dina Yafasova
- *Poetin (Dutch Edition)* by Chris Hutchins and Alexander Korobko
- *A History of Belarus* by Lubov Bazan
- *Children's Fashion of the Russian Empire* by Alexander Vasiliev
- *Empire of Corruption - The Russian National Pastime* by Vladimir Soloviev
- *Heroes of the 90s - People and Money. The Modern History of Russian Capitalism*
- *Fifty Highlights from the Russian Literature (Dutch Edition)* by Maarten Tengbergen
- *Bajesvolk (Dutch Edition)* by Mikhail Khodorkovsky
- *Tsarina Alexandra's Diary (Dutch Edition)*
- *Myths about Russia* by Vladimir Medinskiy
- *Boris Yeltsin - The Decade that Shook the World* by Boris Minaev
- *A Man Of Change - A study of the political life of Boris Yeltsin*
- *Sberbank - The Rebirth of Russia's Financial Giant* by Evgeny Karasyuk
- *To Get Ukraine* by Oleksandr Shyshko
- *Asystole* by Oleg Pavlov
- *Gnedich* by Maria Rybakova
- *Marina Tsvetaeva - The Essential Poetry*
- *Multiple Personalities* by Tatyana Shcherbina
- *The Investigator* by Margarita Khemlin
- *The Exile* by Zinaida Tulub
- *Leo Tolstoy – Flight from paradise* by Pavel Basinsky
- *Moscow in the 1930* by Natalia Gromova
- *Laurus (Dutch edition)* by Evgenij Vodolazkin
- *Prisoner* by Anna Nemzer
- *The Crime of Chernobyl - The Nuclear Goulag* by Wladimir Tchertkoff
- *Alpine Ballad* by Vasil Bykau
- *The Complete Correspondence of Hryhory Skovoroda*

- *The Tale of Aypi* by Ak Welsapar
- *Selected Poems* by Lydia Grigorieva
- *The Fantastic Worlds of Yuri Vynnychuk*
- *The Garden of Divine Songs and Collected Poetry of Hryhory Skovoroda*
- *Adventures in the Slavic Kitchen: A Book of Essays with Recipes*
- *Seven Signs of the Lion* by Michael M. Naydan
- *Forefathers' Eve* by Adam Mickiewicz
- *One-Two* by Igor Eliseev
- *Girls, be Good* by Bojan Babić
- *Time of the Octopus* by Anatoly Kucherena
- *Soghomon Tehlirian Memories - The Assassination of Talaat*
- *The Grand Harmony* by Bohdan Ihor Antonych
- *The Selected Lyric Poetry Of Maksym Rylsky*
- *The Shining Light* by Galymkair Mutanov
- *The Frontier: 28 Contemporary Ukrainian Poets - An Anthology*
- *Acropolis - The Wawel Plays* by Stanisław Wyspiański
- *Contours of the City* by Attyla Mohylny
- *Conversations Before Silence: The Selected Poetry of Oles Ilchenko*
- *Nikolai Gumilev's Africa*
- *Zinnober's Poppets* by Elena Chizhova
- *The Hemingway Game* by Evgeni Grishkovets

More coming soon...